Truth or Dare

Hollyoaks

DO682583

PENGUIN BOOKS

Published by the Penguin Group
Penguin Books Ltd, 80 Strand, London WC2R 0RL, England
Penguin Group (USA) Inc., 375 Hudson Street, New York, New York 10014, USA
Penguin Group (Canada), 90 Eglinton Avenue East, Suite 700, Toronto, Ontario, Canada M4P 2Y3
(a division of Pearson Penguin Canada Inc.)
Penguin Ireland, 25 St Stephen's Green, Dublin 2, Ireland (a division of Penguin Books Ltd)
Penguin Group (Australia), 250 Camberwell Road, Camberwell, Victoria 3124, Australia
(a division of Pearson Australia Group Pty Ltd)
Penguin Books India Pvt Ltd, 11 Community Centre, Panchsheel Park, New Delhi – 110 017, India
Penguin Group (NZ), cnr Airborne and Rosedale Roads, Albany, Auckland 1310, New Zealand
(a division of Pearson New Zealand Ltd)
Penguin Books (South Africa) (Pty) Ltd, 24 Sturdee Avenue, Rosebank,
Johannesburg 2196, South Africa

Penguin Books Ltd, Registered Offices: 80 Strand, London WC2R 0RL, England

penguin.com

First published 2006
1

Set in Avenir Book by Palimpsest Book Production Limited, Polmont, Stirlingshire
Made and printed in England by Clays Ltd, St Ives plc

British Library Cataloguing in Publication Data
A CIP catalogue record for this book is available from the British Library

ISBN-13: 978-0-141-32082-3
ISBN-10: 0-141-32082-6

Truth
or Dare

HOLLYOAKS

ANGELA CORNER

PENGUIN BOOKS

The Big Day

SUNDAY

Hannah

'The coach is late.' Mrs Barnes didn't even look at her watch but she knew exactly what time it was . . . like she had an inbuilt clock ticking away inside her. Probably implanted where her heart should be. A little pang of sadness passed over me, thinking about leaving my Mum for what would be the longest time ever. My Mum might not be uber-glamorous or very organized but at least she was fun. From what Sarah had told me and from what I'd seen, she couldn't wait to get away from hers. I knew Mrs Barnes didn't approve of Sarah spending time with Nancy or me. We were unwanted distractions. But you can't keep best friends apart. That's just inhuman. But what can you expect from someone like Mrs Barnes?

'This is ridiculous. Who organized the trip? Mr Lang? Is that him? I'm going to have a word with him.' Mrs Barnes was all ready to go into battle with Mr Lang. He was pacing at the school gates, looking as worried as everyone else and I wanted to yell and warn him to run while he still could. He was such a softie he wouldn't stand a chance against the hurricane that was Sarah's Mum. We all liked Mr Lang. He took us for General Studies this year but his real subject was history. He told funny jokes and let us have a bit longer for our homework if we came up with a really imaginative excuse that he'd never heard before. Like the time Nancy told him she hadn't done her essay because she'd accidentally glued her hands together and had spent all night in casualty. Along with Nancy's older sister, Mrs Dean, he was the nicest teacher we had. Just a pity Mrs Dean couldn't come with us to France too. Having her and Mr Lang in charge would have been excellent, though with Nancy and Sarah still not talking the holiday had already turned from something we were all excited about to something I was almost dreading.

I didn't even know what they'd fallen out about. Sarah had said it was nothing. And Nancy had said the exact same thing. But they kept giving each other the evils. What sort of holiday would we have if they did that for the entire time? Whatever it was that Nancy and Sarah had argued over I bet it was Nancy who started it. She has this knack of putting her foot in things. If there were a Pop Idol competition for saying the wrong thing at the wrong time she would win it, by a million votes.

'Mum . . . don't. It's nothing to do with him.' Sarah's voice sounded as desperate as I felt. Mrs Barnes stopped in her tracks.

Then, like in a movie, before Mrs Barnes could do anything else, the rumble of a large engine made us all spin round and the coach pulled in through the gates. It squealed to an abrupt stop right in front of us. The doors whistled open to reveal a pair of legs adorned with bright pink socks and familiar chunky Kickers standing on the steps.

'Hi, guys. Anyone need a lift to France?' Nancy beamed at us, like she had single-handedly saved the day. Which I guess, grudgingly, she had. I glanced at Sarah who didn't look too happy to see her. I had to find out what was wrong and get them to make up. It was my mission for the next few days. But, please God, don't let it take that long. I couldn't bear it.

Sarah

It was so like Nancy to make a grand entrance. She always ended up as the centre of attention without even trying. How on earth did she manage to flag down the coach and climb on board before anyone else? I'm convinced she has some sort of lucky gene that makes everything always work out for her. Not like me.

'I've nabbed the back seat for us. Brian will sort your cases out,' Nancy said as we climbed on board. She was on first name terms with the driver already – typical. She hurried down the aisle without waiting for an answer from either of us. Hannah looked at me and shrugged, knowing it was pointless arguing with Nancy in full flow.

'Maybe I should sit somewhere else.'

'Don't be silly. She meant both of us. Come on.'

I was pretty sure Nancy hadn't meant me but it was nice of Hannah to say it.

We all trooped to the back where Nancy plonked herself down like the Queen on her throne. She smiled at Hannah then patted the seat.

'We've got some holiday romances to plan.' She gave me a dirty look. I knew she was having a dig about my so-called romance. Of all the boys in the world why did I have to fall for my best friend's older brother? I wish I could click my fingers and make the feelings go away, but I tried that – I tried for ages to forget about him, and it didn't work. Hannah would go ballistic if she knew I still fancied him and she'd never speak to me again if she knew Rhys and me had been meeting up behind her back. And who could blame her. It was horrible lying to her but I couldn't stop myself, even though according to him we were 'just good friends'.

Maybe a week away in France would help to put him out of my mind. That was the plan anyway. Or at least that was what I kept telling myself.

And if that didn't do the trick spending a week with Nancy giving me the evils should. Somehow she'd found out I'd been meeting Rhys, or maybe it was a lucky guess. But whichever it was she didn't approve. I tried to tell myself it was because she was jealous. She'd fancied Rhys herself when she'd first met him.

But I knew it was because what I was doing wasn't fair on Hannah. The thought of Nancy telling her made me feel sick to the stomach. I was trapped and I couldn't see a way out. A bit like with my swimming. What I wanted to do and what I had to do were very different things.

'You can't plan things like that . . . they either happen or they don't. What's meant to be . . .' Hannah had that dreamy look in her eyes that she always got when talking about boys.

'Will be . . . I know . . . I know. It's all down

5

to fate. But there's nothing wrong with giving fate a little helpful nudge once in a while, is there?'

'Maybe. I'd rather just wait and see what happens. What d'you reckon Sarah?'

I was starting to think if you just sat back and waited then nothing would ever happen.

'Sarah's not the sort to sit around and do nothing.' Nancy didn't look at me but I knew exactly what she was getting at. She could be such a cow. If Nancy even hinted about what she knew, or even what she thought she knew, Hannah would guess that I'd been spending time with Rhys and she'd never speak to me again.

She was my best friend. I'd never had one of those before. Swimming had been my best friend before I'd realized how much I was missing out on. I liked having a living, breathing best friend. I didn't want to lose her or Nancy or Nicole.

But I didn't want to lose him either.

Why did Nancy have to stir things up all the time?

'I wish you two would just start being nice to each other.' Hannah looked at Nancy, then back at me. If only it was that easy.

'That's not up to me, is it?' I gave Nancy what I hoped was a warning glance. She pulled a face and shifted up towards the window as Hannah sat next to her and pulled me down on to the seat.

'Look it's Beaky . . . I didn't think he was coming.' Nancy grinned with excitement and nudged Hannah's arm. 'He fancies you like mad. He's looking over.' Hannah slid down into her seat trying to hide. Tyler 'Beaky' Ackroyd was a complete loser from our year. He was the goalie in the football team and the fact that he was really good at it was his only redeeming feature. He might have a 'thing' for Hannah but it was totally one way. Hannah thought he was repulsive. He had sweaty palms and a pathetic attempt at a goatee. Nowhere close to being Hannah's dream man.

'If you say anything to him, or leave me alone with him I'll kill you. Both of you.'

'But I've heard he's really good with his hands.' Nancy giggled.

'Only if he's got his goalkeeping gloves on.' Hannah gave her a dirty look.

'I'm sure that could be arranged. He might think you were a bit kinky though.' Nancy waved at Beaky who flushed red and sat down right at the front.

'I'm warning you, Nancy.'

'OK . . . OK . . . but we've got to find you someone. You'll be eighteen before you know it and you still haven't done it with anyone.'

'We're not all in a rush.' I heard the words

coming out of my mouth before I could stop myself.

'Oh really?' Nancy looked at me and it was my turn to go red. I turned away and started rummaging in my bag. Nancy turned her attention back to Hannah.

'There's sure to be loads of fit French lads. You're bound to meet someone you fancy. By the law of averages it has to happen eventually.'

Hannah gave her a look. It was true though. I don't think Hannah had fancied any lad in the whole time I'd known her, excluding actors and pop stars that is. She was totally in love with Robbie Williams. But in the real world no one seemed to measure up.

'I'm just saying,' Nancy continued undaunted. 'And French guys are so much fitter than British guys. It's a scientific fact.'

'Yeah, right.' Hannah was still in a huff.

'They sound sexier,' Nancy said. How could anyone argue with that?

'I suppose. Like Thierry Henry.' Hannah was back in dreamworld again, 'I do love the way he speaks. Va va voom . . .' Hannah did her best French accent and grinned, good mood fully restored. 'He is really sexy. I'd love a man like him.'

'I'd love his money.' Typical Nancy.

'Would you go out with someone just because they were loaded?' Hannah was on a roll now. I felt kind of left out but I didn't mind, as long as the topic of conversation stayed well away from Rhys and me. I watched as the coach filled up but kept one ear on the conversation.

'Why not? But they'd have to be fit as well though.' Nancy thought for a moment. 'And definitely no pensioners. I don't care who they are or what they do.'

'Seems fair. So how about you and Brian the coach driver? Look, he's smiling at you.' Hannah pointed out of the window to where Brian was throwing the last of the cases on to the coach.

Nancy took the bait and peered out. Brian just happened to look up at that moment. He winked. Nancy jolted back to her seat.

'Oh, my God.'

'Not your type then, Nance?'

'I'd rather join a convent.' Nancy narrowed her eyes. 'But we're all going to get at least a bit of va va voom while we're in France. If you know what I mean.'

'It would be nice to meet someone, I suppose.' Hannah sighed.

'Then we'll have to find you a nice French guy. Leave it to me.'

Hannah looked to me for help. When Nancy

said she was going to sort something out she always did. If Hannah wanted a French guy then Nancy would find her one. Scary thought. Whoever Nancy found was unlikely to be the man of Hannah's dreams because the man of her dreams only existed in her imagination. Maybe it was time she did the unthinkable and settled for someone less than perfect. I couldn't imagine Hannah ever doing that though. And I had no room to talk. I'd already found my perfect man who I was nowhere near ready to give up on. Hannah was an optimist. She would keep dreaming, especially when there was a whole new country in front of us, with a whole new set of possibilities.

'Worth giving it a try?' I replied. It felt very lame.

'Well, if we're going to find someone for me we'll have to find someone for you too.' Hannah sounded determined. 'What sort of guy do you want? Tall, dark and handsome?'

The smile froze on my face as I felt Nancy's glare burn on to my cheek.

'I . . . erm . . . I don't know . . .'

'Some people just aren't that fussy,' Nancy muttered. Hannah looked at her, then back at me. It was so obvious something was horribly wrong, but she just looked thoughtful and before she could investigate further Mr Lang yelled for us all to be quiet so he could take the register. The coach was full and even Brian had climbed on board and shut the door. I looked at my watch. We were nearly an hour late already. If we missed the ferry no one would be finding a man, of any description. But at least I wouldn't be away from Rhys. My one hope was that absence did make the heart grow fonder and that when I got back Rhys would have missed me so much he would decide being friends wasn't enough. It wasn't only Hannah who could dream of happy endings.

Hannah

I'd forgotten to take my travel sickness tablets. I only remembered when we were about to drive on to the Eurotunnel train. By then I was already feeling sick and of course they take twenty minutes to start working. I was still feeling weird when we hit French soil at the other side. The only thing that made me feel a bit better was the fact that the château was only another hour or so away. Sarah and Nancy had both fallen asleep. Even after being stuck together in a little metal tube for so many hours they hadn't started talking. Not really. They'd both been dropping snide little comments, but still neither would let on about what they'd fallen out over. Could two people be more infuriating?

I can never get to sleep on a coach. It's just so uncomfortable. In fact I think only Brian and me were still awake as we drove through northern France. Lucky really as he was the one doing the driving. I wasn't sure whether it was to keep himself awake but he seemed to aim for every single bump on the road. Either that or he was doing it on purpose because Mr Lang had a go at him for being late. It was the first time I'd ever heard him raise his voice. Even Miss O'Donnell looked surprised. I'd hoped she wouldn't be too much of a pain over the next few days. It would have been much better if Mrs Dean had come with us. Miss O'Donnell is a right miserable old cow. She's well into her thirties and still single, so I suppose it's not surprising she's got a face like a grumpy old terrier. That's what Nancy said, anyway, and she gets all the inside info from her sister.

I stared at my reflection in the window. Maybe I shouldn't bitch about Miss O'Donnell. At the rate I was going I'd probably end up just like her.

It was such a horrible thought I pushed it straight out of my head and decided instead that in the next four days I would meet a really gorgeous French boy.

He'd look like Orlando Bloom and sound like Thierry Henry. We'd fall madly in love the moment our eyes met, and even though we spoke different languages we'd know exactly what the other one was saying and thinking. He'd be called Jean Claude . . . or maybe Pascal. His parents would be related to French royalty – if they hadn't all got their heads chopped off in the Revolution.

Anyway, he'd live in a beautiful château and write poetry and on our last night together he'd declare his undying love for me. We'd get engaged – secretly of course . . . though I'd tell Sarah – and when I'd done my A-levels and my degree we'd move into an apartment in Paris and have lots of beautiful babies together.

If he was out there Nancy would find him. I still couldn't believe how she'd talked herself on to the coach. Her and the driver seemed like old pals – he even gave her first choice of the DVDs he put on. Of course, Nancy being Nancy chose *Reservoir Dogs*. Miss O'Donnell flipped out when it got to the ear-slicing bit. She nearly fell off her seat.

I couldn't blame her, though. It was pretty disgusting. The lads were all cheering at the screen, though. Sad or what? I don't see what's so entertaining about watching someone's ear get cut off. Brian put on *Four Weddings and a Funeral* after that, which is one of my favourite films. Hugh Grant is so cute in it and there's a happy ending. Nancy has horrible taste in movies. If it doesn't involve at least one body part being removed she's not interested.

I wish I could twist men around my little finger as well as she does, though. And she is so cool without even needing to try. Like the way the coach doors opened and she was there on the steps like a superhero saving the day. Only Nancy could do something like that. I wished I could be more like her . . . take chances . . . be spontaneous. I have my whole life planned out. I even have it all written down in the back of my diary (that part that says 'Notes' that nobody I know, apart from me, has ever used) – my life plan for the next twenty years. University next year to study English. While I'm there I'll meet the love of my life. He'll be very good looking, but intelligent, funny, sensitive, and a great cook. We won't get married until we've both graduated and got amazing jobs in London. But when we do it'll be in a beautiful little country church with the reception in a huge, very tastefully decorated marquee. My dress will be white, with a huge train, designed just for me. We'll buy a lovely big house in Notting Hill, with varnished floorboards and huge windows. We'll get two kittens, called

Ant and Dec, and go skiing in the winter and to Mauritius in the summer. When I've become really successful in my job I will get pregnant. I'll give up work and have three children, two girls and a boy – Anise, Riana and Jeremiah . . . I could go on and on.

I'd never let anyone see it, not even my best friends, but every so often I flick to the back pages and remind myself what I've got planned. I read somewhere once that if you write something down it's more likely to come true. I hope so. My life is so far from perfect now it can only get better.

Still, compared to some people, my life is brilliant. Nicole, for instance. She's had such an awful time in the last few weeks. I don't even know all the details. She cries a lot, though, and I wish I could do something to make her feel better. But what do you say to someone who's been attacked like that? She has nightmares about Andy all the time. I know her Mum is really worried about her and wants her to go and see someone to talk about it. I wish she'd talk to me. I really miss her. Things aren't the same without her around. And she's the only one of us not afraid to stand up to Nancy. By the time the coach had driven out of Chester she'd have found out what Sarah and Nancy had argued about and got them to make friends.

I got my mobile out and sent her a text. Five minutes later my phone bleeped.

Missing you too.

I smiled to myself. Maybe she just needed a bit of time to get over things and one day, in the not too distant future, we'd get the old Nicole back. But for now it was up to me to sort the Nancy problem out. Even though I had no idea where to start.

Nancy

'Urghh . . . it's not exactly picture postcard is it?' I stared out of the window, wishing I'd never fallen asleep. I had a crick in my neck and I could feel a headache coming on. It didn't help that the countryside outside the coach window was flat, muddy and tired looking. Little grey concrete box houses dotted the fields and rain ran in huge rivers down the windows. The only other buildings that seemed to be out there were wine supermarkets, loads of them. Not how I'd imagined France. Where were the pretty villages, the delicatessens and the big châteaux? And not one single moustached man on a bike with a string of garlic around his neck. In fact, I wasn't that convinced we'd left England at all.

Hannah looked up from her book. She was

reading *Bridget Jones's Diary*. Again. Like it was realistic for Bridget to worry about her weight when she was way under 10 stone for the entire story. That makes Bridget a size 12 at most — hardly a whale.

'It's not supposed to be pretty round here. It's the Somme.'

'And?'

'You know . . . where millions of people got killed in the First World War. Trenches, acres of mud, barbed wire . . .'

'I knew that.' I did too, though I always got mixed up between world wars . . . who fought what, where. 'I hope it's a bit nicer where we're staying. What's it called again, Valley or something?'

'Vailly. Just near there anyway. It's supposed to be lovely. One of the undiscovered corners of France.' Hannah shut up suddenly and went red.

'Have you been Googling again?'

She nodded.

'I just wanted to know where we were going.'

'I know where we're going. Some cold, spooky château in the middle of nowhere.'

'Well, I'm going to have a good time even if you're not.'

I felt bad then. I was snappy because of my headache. And because I wished Sarah hadn't fallen out with me.

'Just ignore me. We *will* have a good time. And I bet the château is straight out of a fairy tale.'

Hannah smiled at that. I looked across to where Sarah was still sleeping. She was smiling, just a little, and I wondered if she was dreaming of Rhys. If it wasn't for the opposite sex I bet we'd never fall out at all.

'What's up with you and Sarah?'

For a horrible moment I thought Hannah could read my mind.

'Nothing.'

She gave me a look.

'We just had a stupid argument. I can't even remember what it was about.'

'If it was just something stupid why don't you make up?'

'Why does it always have to be me who makes the first move?'

'Because it's normally you who causes the argument in the first place.'

Not this time. If Hannah knew what I knew she'd be right on my side. It really wasn't fair at all. I'd been trying to help Sarah, but she'd taken it all the wrong way. Like I was trying to blackmail her or something, which I totally wasn't. I'd just said if she liked Rhys she should be honest and tell Hannah how she felt. Hannah would go ballistic, but at least she'd know and maybe one day she'd come round to the idea. Unlikely, but you never know. Sarah just flatly denied there was anything going on, but I'm not stupid. I've seen the way she looks at him, and him at her. She should just admit it or forget him and get on with her life.

'Thanks a lot.' I turned back to the window, starting to wish I had gone back home and hidden in my bedroom for the week.

'I'm just saying. I don't like being stuck in the middle.'

A signpost to Vailly flashed by the window.

'Isn't that where we're going?' I was glad of the distraction. It worked perfectly. Hannah seemed to forget the argument and slid up closer to the window to look. She grinned at me. We were almost there. I could worry about Sarah later. Why do something today when you can put it off until tomorrow?

Sarah

Have you ever had one of those amazing, perfect dreams that make you so happy you never want to wake up? And when you do wake up you try to make yourself go straight back to sleep again so you can carry on with the dream, but of course you never can. My dream was about Rhys . . . of course. He was telling me how much he loved me and how we'd be together forever. Hannah was there too, and she was so happy that Rhys and me were together. She said how great it would be to have me as a sister . . . even if it was only by law. Nancy was in the dream, too. That wasn't so nice. She was running some evil detective agency. She looked just like Bad Willow in *Buffy the Vampire Slayer*, with her eyes all black and veins standing out on her face. She kept yelling at me that she wanted Rhys for herself and that I'd never be able to keep him. Then me, Hannah and Rhys were all being chased and running really fast, and we got to these big, gold gates belonging to a huge, pink castle. The gates swung open to let us in and shut behind us so Bad Nancy couldn't follow. We heard her screaming and yelling, but there was nothing she could do. Behind the gates it was paradise: beautiful gardens full of white roses, a river of gold flowing down to a waterfall. We were so happy and relieved to have escaped. It was an amazing feeling. Then Rhys got down on one knee to propose to me and it felt like my heart would burst with happiness.

I snapped out of my dream, just at the moment Rhys was about to say 'Will you marry me?', to see Hannah grinning at me and prodding my arm.

'We're here.'

I frowned. I couldn't help it. She couldn't have chosen a worse moment to wake me up. I wanted that incredible happy feeling back.

'I can't believe you've slept almost the entire way.' She didn't seem to notice my frown. 'Look you can see the roof of the château. It's got turrets and everything.'

She pointed out of the window. Nancy was looking out, too, and thinking of her as Bad Nancy cheered me up a little.

Everyone on the coach had their eyes glued to what was outside. We disappeared into a wood, the branches leaning down so low that they scraped the roof of the coach in places. A couple of the other girls, Kelly and Natalie, down at the front of the coach, screamed.

'Oh, I'm so scared,' Nancy yelled at them. 'We're all going to get molested by leaves.'

They gave her the evils back but that made Hannah giggle even more, and I couldn't help but smile.

Then the coach came out of the woods and in front of us was Château Morne.

'Oh, my God.' Hannah's eyes went really wide. 'It's beautiful.'

'It's pink.' Nancy was less impressed.

It was beautiful, though. Like something out of a Disney movie. It was sort of pink. Not bright pink or anything, but what one of Mum's posh interior design magazines would call 'salmon'. It had six giant turrets, with narrow slits for windows, and a lake in front of it that reflected a perfect mirror image. It was spookily like the castle in my dream.

'I bet loads of people have fallen in love here. It's so romantic,' Hannah said, without taking her eyes off the château.

'More likely it's haunted by the ghost of some woman who was betrayed by her scheming, violent husband and threw herself off the top of that turret in despair.'

'Where did that come from?' Hannah dragged her eyes away from the view just long enough to pull a face at Nancy.

'Fact: these old piles always have a tragic history.'

'Not always.'

'Yes. Always. You don't get centuries of history without at least some horrible deaths and suicides thrown in. And when you get a bunch of rich people living together it's even more likely to end in blood and guts.'

'Not here. I just know it's a happy place. I can

feel it.' Hannah looked at me, wanting me to back her up. The pink castle in my dream was definitely a happy place and I figured that was close enough.

'It's lovely. I don't see how anyone could be miserable living here.'

Hannah smiled, and nodded at Nancy.

'See. I bet we'll all fall in love while we're here. Even you.'

Nancy raised an eyebrow. 'What's love got to do with anything? I'm only interested in lust.'

'Whatever.' Hannah gave me a look. I don't think she believed anyone could be in lust without there being some love involved. I believed it, though. I had to. Rhys had this on–off thing with a girl at college. I'd never asked him about it – I didn't dare – but I'd overheard her talking about him to one of her friends. She said that it was just a lust thing, for both of them. I hoped it was true. She was really pretty and the same age as him. It made me feel sick to think of them together, but as long as he didn't love her that was OK . . . right? I wish I could talk to someone about it, ask their opinion, but there isn't anyone. Nicole is the only person I could have asked, but how could I bother her after what she'd been through? My problems seem pathetic in comparison to hers. I wished she had come with us, though. It was better when there were four of us. With three people someone always gets left out.

Hannah

'There are rooms for two people or rooms for three people. Which do you want?' Miss Rousseau, the Accommodation Manager, stared at us, clipboard in hand. She looked like the identical twin of that French actress in *Amélie*, except her hair was much longer and tied back into a ponytail. She was also much more intimidating than the girl in the film. I smiled at her. She just stared back, waiting for an answer. I dropped my gaze, right down to the floor. She had on great shoes, bought on the Champs-Élysées, I decided. If this were Chester she'd be wearing something flat and sensible, with scuffed toes. I liked France already. You can tell a lot about a person from what they wear on their feet. I let my eyes drift across to Nancy's Kickers, and then to Sarah and her ankle boots that were totally 2004. It was probably shallow to judge people by footwear.

'Come on. I haven't got all day.' It was weird hearing a French accent speaking such perfect English. She spoke better English than most of the lads in our year. But then most of them couldn't manage much more than a Neanderthal grunt while scratching their armpits and rearranging their dangly bits.

I looked at Sarah and Nancy, but neither was making any move to answer. I knew they wouldn't want to share a room, but how was I supposed to choose between them?

'What is the problem? There are three of you . . . so you want a room for three?' She studied our faces. 'You have argued?'

I just shrugged helplessly. Miss Rousseau narrowed her eyes. She looked at Nancy, who was paying close attention to her nails, and then at Sarah, who seemed to be finding the view out of the window very interesting.

'I will solve your problem for you. I have a room for three right here. It's now yours.' She opened a door behind her. I could see three beds packed into a small room, a cavernous looking wardrobe and a washbasin.

'But . . .' Sarah started to protest.

Miss Rousseau silenced her with one look before continuing. 'The bathroom is at the end of the hall. All guests are expected back in their rooms by midnight, unless permission has been granted otherwise. My room is the first one on the right. If you want me, please knock, but it had better be for a very good reason or I will be extremely unhappy. Enjoy your stay.'

She ticked a box on her papers and clipped away down the hall to the next group.

'Who wants the bed by the window?' I asked.

'I'll have it.' Nancy grabbed the handle of her bag and, before either of us could argue, headed into the room, flinging herself on to the bed.

'Can I have the bed nearest the door?' Sarah looked at me. 'So I won't disturb you when I get up early to go and do my training?'

'I thought you said you were going to skip training this week.'

'I can't. Not really. Mum will know when I get back if I haven't been swimming.' She shrugged, 'So is it OK? About the bed?'

'Of course.'

She smiled and went into the room. I followed her and stood at the end of my bed. The one in the middle.

Nancy

As soon as Sarah went off to check out the swimming pool I knew Hannah was going to have a go at me. My earphones were rammed into my ears as far as was humanly possible and Franz was turned up as loud as I could bear without my brain imploding. I even lay on my side with my back to the room and shut my eyes, but I could still feel her gaze burrowing into me. I couldn't cope any longer. I tugged my headphones out and flipped over.

'OK . . . what is it? Say what you've got to say.'

'Why are you being so horrible to Sarah?' Now she had my attention she went back to putting her clothes on the hangers in the wardrobe.

'Ask her. Anyway I'm not being horrible.'

'What do you call ignoring her then?'

'I'm not ignoring her. I just don't have anything to say. There's a difference.'

Hannah gave me one of her unimpressed looks. I pulled a face back.

'Why aren't you having a go at her?'

'Because I'm having a go at you.'

'Yeah, well, don't expect me to stay and listen.' I got up, but I couldn't go anywhere. The combination of bed, Hannah and gigantic wardrobe meant my exit was well and truly blocked.

'You should be nicer to her.'

'I haven't done anything.'

'She did something to you then? What was it? Tell me.'

'Not to me . . .'

'What does that mean?'

For a moment, a very short moment, I thought

about telling her. That Sarah was in love with her older brother, the brother she'd sworn blue, black and red she no longer had feelings for and would never go anywhere near because her friendship with Hannah meant so much more to her than any stupid boy crush.

'Nothing.'

'She's had a tough time, you know . . . with her Dad giving up work and everything . . . They might have to sell their house . . . move some-where smaller. Plus her Mum gives her so much stick. She doesn't ever let up on her, everything's about swimming. Nothing else matters. I'm sure her Mum would prefer it if she didn't have friends at all.'

'I know.' Sarah's Mum was a nightmare. Mine was no laugh a minute either but I didn't have to live with her. I got to live with my sister, who was pretty cool, when she wasn't nagging me to tidy up or to stop annoying Chewbacca (my old nickname for Jake because he's the world's hairiest living man – a scientific marvel).

'And she was so happy when she was allowed to come to France. Her Mum's never let her do anything like this before. You know how much she went on and on about it. How excited she was, how much she was looking forward to it . . . And then you two have to fall out. She even thought about not coming because of you. Did you know that?'

Hannah glared at me. I glared back.

'So are you going to apologize to her?'

'Is she going to apologize to me?'

'I give up. You are so unreasonable, sometimes. This whole holiday is going to be one big disaster and it's your fault. I don't even know why I'm friends with you half the time.' Hannah spun on her heel and stormed out of the room.

I sank down on to the bed. I didn't want it to be like this. Sarah wasn't the only one who'd been looking forward to this holiday, and Hannah wasn't the only one hoping to have themselves a holiday romance. It had been so long since someone I fancied had actually been interested in me as a person I'd almost forgotten what it felt like. I mean, lots of lads tried to get off with me, but that's not the same thing. Sometimes it's nice to talk and have a laugh. Yeah, I know, that doesn't sound like me at all, but people are full of surprises, if you just look a bit closer.

Sarah

I thought having a swim might make me feel a bit better, but I couldn't concentrate. All I could think about was what Rhys was doing and whether he was thinking of me. As soon as I climbed out of the pool I checked my mobile to see if he'd texted me. He hadn't, of course. I sent him one, saying we'd arrived safely and that I wished he were here with me. I didn't send it. But I didn't delete it either. I was already really missing him. The thought of not seeing him for four whole days was horrible.

He had told me to text him whenever I could, and he'd lent me a CD by one of his favourite bands, Arcade Fire. Both things made me feel better. Having the CD meant I could take a little bit of him with me, even if his taste in music was a tad weird.

'They use all sorts of weird things as percussion. Kitchen pans, old rusty radiators. They're seriously cool,' he'd said, with a totally straight face.

He was a drummer, so he was into that sort of thing. But to me most of the music he liked was just noise. I'd never have told him that. I was so happy just to have one of his CDs to take with me that I had to force myself to stop grinning like an idiot. I decided I would listen to Arcade Fire until they sounded good. Even if my ears started to bleed.

The last thing he'd said to me before I'd said

goodbye was the best thing of all. He'd told me to stay away from the local lads. That had to mean something. At least I knew he cared about me a little bit.

I went back to the room planning on playing Arcade Fire and ignoring Nancy, but when I got there Nancy had disappeared. Hannah told me it was probably because she'd had a go at her. It made me feel even guiltier when Hannah said not to worry because she was definitely on my side – which obviously meant Nancy hadn't said anything. I was turning into this really horrible sneaky person. Is learning how to lie and cheat part of growing up? I mean, Dad did it by giving up his job without telling Mum, and you always hear about movie stars cheating on each other. People are at it all the time, lying to their friends, cheating on their partners. I didn't want to be that kind of person.

'You look beautiful.' Hannah said, putting the finishing touches to my hair. We were getting ready to go to the château's welcome barbecue. I looked at my reflection in the mirror with hers smiling over my shoulder. I thought to myself, mirror, mirror on the wall, who is the biggest liar of all?

'Cheer up. I told you not to worry about Nancy.

We'll both give her the silent treatment until she comes crawling for us to forgive her. And I mean really crawling. On her knees.' Hannah nodded. 'Come on, we're late.'

She grabbed my hand and dragged me out of the room.

Downstairs in the dining hall all the chairs and tables were piled next to the walls and a crowd of people, some from our school, others I didn't recognize, were standing about. A DJ booth was set up in one corner, but no one had plucked up the courage to start dancing even though the music was so loud all the teachers were standing outside near the barbecue. I could see Mr Lang juggling with a paper cup and a hotdog, while trying to coax some tomato sauce out of a squeezy bottle. Miss O'Donnell rushed up to help him. The way he smiled at her made me wonder if they had a thing going.

'Hannah . . . are Mr Lang and Miss O'Donnell . . . ?'

'Yeah. Didn't you know? He's far too nice for her. He could do much better. Maybe we should try and set him up with Miss Rousseau . . . she's much prettier.'

'I don't think we should be getting involved with our teachers' love lives.'

'You're probably right. Just thinking about

them having love lives makes me want to throw up.' She grinned. 'You hungry?'

Thing was with Hannah, she always looked on the bright side of every situation.

By the time we'd attacked the barbecue, got some drinks – non-alcoholic unfortunately – and visited the loos a couple of times Nancy still hadn't made an appearance. Hannah decided she was probably off somewhere making voodoo dolls of the both of us. Anyway, we had more important things to think about, like checking out the lads from the other schools.

'He's all right,' she said, and kind of bobbed her head. I couldn't tell where she was looking, but there was a group of five lads staring in our direction. They weren't exactly boy band material.

'Which one?' I looked back to Hannah. She started bouncing on the spot and squealing.

'He's coming over. He's coming over.'

My stomach lurched.

'What?' I turned round, but it was too late. One of the lads was walking in our direction. He reminded me of Seth Cohen from the OC but with spiky hair that must have taken him ages to get right and, I guess, he did have quite a nice smile. He glanced at Hannah, but stared straight at me.

'I couldn't borrow your mobile phone, could I?' He had an accent straight off *Eastenders*.

Hannah and I looked at each other. She gave me an encouraging nudge.

'What for?'

'I want to call my Mum and tell her I've just met the girl of my dreams.' He said it with a completely straight face. Hannah and me burst out laughing.

'What? Was that bad?' He did this goofy grin thing and slapped himself on the forehead, 'I'm such an idiot sometimes. I am so sorry. Can you find it in your . . .' he paused and took a mini-step back, as if overwhelmed by something, 'wow . . . in your incredibly beautiful heart to forgive me?'

'Yeah . . . I guess.' I noticed he was wearing a green Firetrap shirt. Rhys had one just like it.

'You will? Thank God. My life would have been over if you hadn't.' He grinned, glanced back at his mates, who were still staring, and mouthed the words 'I think I'm in love.'

'He's cute isn't he? I think he really likes you,' Hannah whispered in my ear, 'I'll be over there if you need me.'

'What? No . . . I need you now . . .' But it was too late, the music was too loud for her to hear me and she'd already started to walk off. I made a grab for her arm but missed and she slipped away into the crowd.

'Looks like it's just you and me. I'm Murphy by the way.' He looked at me and waited.

'Oh . . . I'm Sarah.' I looked over his shoulder, desperate to catch Hannah's eye, but she had her back to me, talking to a couple of the other girls from our year.

'So am I really forgiven for the cheesy chat-up line?'

'I've heard worse.'

'I suppose you must get hundreds of guys trying it on . . . I'm just one in a long line of hopeless wannabes.' For a moment he looked so downcast I almost felt sorry for him, and then he grinned again. 'So is it a yes or a no?'

I couldn't help but smile back. He was one of those people who when they smiled you had no choice but to join in.

'It's a no, isn't it? I can tell. You've got a boyfriend, haven't you? Of course you have . . . no one who looks as good as you could be single. Story of my life . . . always runner up, never the winner.' He shrugged. 'I guess I'll see you around, Smiler.'

He turned to walk off, but hesitated and leant in closer so he could whisper in my ear.

'And thanks for talking to me . . . my mates thought you'd blow me out straight off. You made me look pretty cool.'

And with that he was gone. I stared after him, not quite sure what I felt. He was actually nice and not unfanciable. In any other life I might have been interested, but not in this one. Pity a certain person hadn't been here to see me getting chatted up.

'Well? What happened?' Hannah was suddenly standing next to me. I had no idea where she'd sprung from. 'Did he ask you out? I can't believe you've pulled already and it's only the first night.'

'I haven't pulled anyone.'

'He fancied you, though.'

'I suppose.'

'And you fancied him?'

'Not really.'

'Why not? He's the buffest lad in the room. By miles.'

'I don't know. I just didn't.'

'Your Mum's not here now, you know. You are allowed a boyfriend.'

'It's not that.'

'What is it then?'

What if I just told her . . . here and now? Explained that I wasn't interested in Murphy because I was still in love with her brother and that I was really sorry but you can't help who you fall in love with. She should understand that. She's the one who believes in fate and destiny.

I'd almost psyched myself up to blurt it out,

I'd even got as far as starting to open my mouth, when someone shoved me in the back and sent me flying. I got my balance back and turned round to protest to the person who'd bumped into me, expecting them to say sorry. But the person standing in front of me looked anything but sorry.

'Bitch.' The girl spat the word at me. I even felt her spit on my face. She was my height, kind of pretty in a scary 'I'm going to smash your face in' way. She had a one of those tattoo bands round the top of each arm. She definitely wasn't happy and I had no idea what I'd done.

'Pardon?' I could see Hannah out of the corner of my eye. She looked as terrified as I felt.

'If you go near Murphy again I'll rip your eyes out. Got that?'

'He came up to me.' I knew as soon as I spoke I should have kept my mouth shut.

'You want to start something with me?'

'No . . . I . . .' I glanced at Hannah for help, but we were both way out of our depth.

'Come on then . . .' She shoved me backwards with her hand. 'Let's see what you've got.'

'I wouldn't do that if I were you.' Suddenly Nancy was there, looking as hard as nails. I'd never been more pleased to see anyone in my life. The girl spun round to see who owned the voice.

'Oh . . . You are as ugly as you sound.' Nancy slowly looked her up and down, 'Nice dress, though. Are you hoping you'll slim into it one day?'

'Who are you?' The girl growled at her but her confidence was shaken. Hannah and I stood shoulder to shoulder behind her, feeling brave now Nancy was there.

'I don't know what your problem is, darling, but I'll bet it's hard to pronounce. Now run along, go bark at someone else.'

They eyeballed each other, Nancy not wavering for a moment. The girl looked away first.

'Whatever.' She glanced back at me, 'Just stay away from Murphy . . . and that goes for anyone else from your chavy school.'

She gave me the evils and went off without another word.

'Thanks, Nancy . . . she'd have battered me if you hadn't turned up.' I really was grateful. My heart was still thundering.

'Too many freaks, not enough circuses.' Nancy shrugged as cool as anything, like she chased off psychos every day of the week. 'Who's this Murphy person, anyway?'

'A lad from another school. He came and chatted Sarah up. Maybe she's his girlfriend or something. She's a right nutter anyway.' Hannah looked like she wanted to hug her.

Nancy looked at me. Then she smiled. She didn't need to say anything. I knew we were friends again.

'Come on. I want to dance.' She linked arms with the both of us and we headed for the centre of the dance floor.

Nancy

I liked riding in to save the day. I still thought Sarah was in the wrong not telling Hannah about Rhys, but there was no way I would let anyone bully my mates. That girl was a right cow but like with all bullies the moment someone stood up to her she ran away like a frightened guinea pig.

I had another reason to feel all pleased with myself. I knew how much Hannah loved shopping and that she might forgive me a little bit if I did something nice for her. While they'd been getting ready for the barbecue, I'd been on the Internet and checked the train times. We were only an hour away from Paris and some of the best shops in the world. It would be dead easy to slip out of the château and get on the train at the village station. We'd be in Paris, do some shopping and get back before anyone even knew we were gone. It was too good an opportunity to miss.

'But Paris . . . it's miles away.' Hannah looked unsure.

'Not that far. Not by train. It'll be easy. What could go wrong?'

'Everything.' Hannah shrugged as we walked back to our room after the barbecue wound up.

'How? We get on a train. Go shopping, check out the sights, eat some pancakes. Then we get the train straight back. Sounds simple.'

'I guess.' Sarah smiled at me. I think she was just glad we were friends again and I clearly wasn't going to say anything about Rhys. 'Could we really get away with it?'

'No problem. We're on holiday. We can do what we like. Come on. It'll be fun. Isn't that why we're here? We'd never get chance to do anything like this back home.'

Hannah thought for a moment. I could see her weighing up the pros and cons. She nodded.

'You're right. I've always dreamed of going to Paris. And we are so close by.'

'So is that a yes? Are we agreed? Wednesday we go to Paris?'

Hannah glanced at Sarah, Sarah glanced at me, then back at Hannah and nodded. Hannah grinned.

'We're going to Paris.' She squeaked with excitement and we all hugged each other. I was just glad we were all friends again. The plan had worked perfectly.

Hannah

I didn't really understand what had happened but I didn't care. Nancy and Sarah were friends again. The rest of the barbecue was a laugh, though we stayed well clear of Murphy and the bitchy girl, who were congregated at one side of the room in a group from their school. Nancy found out her name was Stacy and immediately christened her Schizoid Stacy. She gave us plenty of evils and Murphy looked over at Sarah a lot but nothing else bad happened. We were all disappointed by the lack of male talent. Apart from Murphy there really was no one worth going with. Can you believe we'd come all this way and no fit lads? But we hadn't seen any of the local lads yet, though, so I wasn't about to give up hope. Plus we had the trip to Paris to look forward to. I have to admit a big part of me thought it was a bad idea. But that was the 'childish, have to obey the rules, don't do anything scary' part of me that was determined to have left back in Hollyoaks. Nancy was right. How could we not go, and with her in charge, we'd be OK. She could cope with anything.

'I reckon we're just like the girls in *Sex and the City*,' Nancy said as she flopped down next to me on my bed. Sarah was brushing her teeth at the sink.

'Except they're all really glamorous and have great apartments in New York,' I had to point out, in the interests of reality.

'And fab jobs,' Sarah said as she joined us on the bed.

'Apart from that. We're four best friends – well, one of us is missing, but normally we would be four.'

'And we are going to be friends forever.' I was starting to warm to the subject. I loved *Sex and the City*. I wanted a life like that. But I didn't want to be in my forties before I settled down. *Sex and the City* as a twenty-something sounded better.

'Even if we fall out sometimes.' Sarah smiled at Nancy.

'We know we'll always make up in the end.' Nancy smiled back. I wanted to cry. I loved it when people made up . . . in films and in real life. Nothing made me cry at the cinema more than those making-up scenes.

'Carrie and Miranda fall out all the time,' I said. 'Like when Carrie decided to go to Paris with the Russian.'

'So which of us is which?' Sarah asked.

'I want to be Carrie,' said Nancy, nodding. 'She's the funniest and she's a writer. And she wears whatever she wants.'

'I see you more as a Samantha.' I grinned and thumped her arm. 'Sassy, sexy and really confident with men.'

'Hey . . . I don't sleep around.'

'In Chester it would be sleeping around; in New York it's cool.'

'I can live with that. And she does end up with the fittest guy.'

'Who are you, Sarah?' I looked at her trying to imagine which character she was most like.

'I don't know . . . what d'you think? Just don't say Miranda.'

'You are very successful in what you do . . . and you're ambitious.' That sounded like a Miranda to me.

'I know . . . but no one ever wants to be Miranda.'

'I like Miranda. You should be happy to be her. She earns loads of money, manages a career and a baby and still looks beautiful.'

'OK, then.' Sarah seemed convinced. 'What about you, Hannah?'

'There's only one person I could be . . .'

Sarah and Nancy exchanged glances and then, in unison . . . 'Charlotte.'

'But please don't let me end up with a short, bald guy with a hairy back.'

Nancy pulled a horrified face and we all started laughing. It somehow turned into a pillow fight . . . we all clubbed each other until we were exhausted.

'I think we should make a pledge,' Nancy said as she flopped down on her bed. 'We've got four days away from our families and all the crap back home. We should make the most of every second. Forget whatever's gone on back there . . . none of that matters while we're in a foreign country . . . We should concentrate on being here, right now. Best friends sticking together and having a laugh.'

'That's probably the most sensible thing you've ever said.' I grinned at her.

'Do you think we *can* forget all that other stuff?' Sarah rolled over and crashed on her own bed.

'We can do anything we want.' Nancy smiled at her, 'We're the *Sex and the City* girls. Independently minded, intelligent women who never let men come between them.'

They shared a look. Whatever they'd fallen out over had been well and sorted. I crashed back on to my pillow and stared up at the ceiling. I don't think I'd ever felt so happy and contented in my whole life.

Nancy

I shook Hannah's shoulder really hard. When she slept she really slept.

'What?' she croaked eventually.

'Get up.'

'What time is it?' She squinted at her alarm clock. It was 2.30am. 'Oh, my God. What's happening? Is there a fire or something?'

'Just get up.'

I left her muttering under her duvet and went to wake Sarah. One whisper in her ear and she was wide awake.

They both glared at me.

'Explain. Quick.' Hannah was so grumpy when you woke her up.

'There's a party going on in the turret room. Lizzie knocked on the door as she went past to tell me.' Lizzie was one of the girls in our class. We didn't really hang out with her – she was in all the lower sets, but she was OK. 'It's a first night tradition apparently. We have to go.'

It took a lot more convincing to get them out of bed and heading to the turret room, but I can pretty much persuade anyone to do anything when I put my mind to it. I guess they thought they'd never get any sleep until they agreed to come with me.

The turret room was up a million flights of steps. Hannah and me were knackered by the time we got to the top. For Sarah it was more like an afternoon stroll. She looked at me.

'Are you sure about this?'

'Of course,' I said, between deep inhales of oxygen, 'Come on.'

I pushed open the door and inside the room were a bunch of people from our school. Beaky looked up the moment we stepped inside. He smiled then went red, seeing Hannah. Hannah, seeing him, gave me the evillest look ever. If I hadn't been holding on to her arm she would have done a runner.

'We're on holiday. We are going to have fun,' I whispered in her ear. Sarah shrugged. We were staying put.

Cans of lager and Diet Coke littered the floor. Someone had brought Pringles. It wasn't much of a party, to be fair, but alcohol equalled party to me, so we helped ourselves to some wine.

A while later, when there was more alcohol in our bodies than left in the bottles and cans, someone suggested a game of truth or dare. We all gathered round in a circle. Hannah opened her mouth to protest, but I didn't give her the chance. I grabbed her arm and dragged her to sit down. Sarah followed. She didn't look too happy either. Was I the only spontaneous person here?

'Do you want to spin?' Beaky nudged me.

I grinned, ignoring the evil stare of Hannah burning holes in my shoulder. I grabbed the bottle and gave it a huge flick with my wrist.

It span and span and span and eventually stopped, pointing at Beaky. To be more accurate it stopped between Beaky and his mate Snagger, but Beaky took the initiative.

'Dare,' he said. He'd obviously had a few lagers already. His eyes darted to Hannah, then back to me. It didn't go unnoticed. Hannah pinched my arm so hard I actually squealed.

'OK, then . . .' I said rubbing my arm, 'I dare you to . . .'

I did a sideways glance at Hannah, just to wind her up.

'I dare you to . . . do a moonie out of the window.'

Beaky blinked at me as if I'd told him to jump out of the window, not just wave his backside out of it. Everyone else was laughing.

'No way,' he stuttered.

'You asked for the dare. You have to do it. Who's going to see anyway?'

He looked at me, to see if I was serious. I was. He thought for a moment, then got up, backed up to the window, dropped his kegs down at the back and did a moonie. From where we were sitting we couldn't see a thing.

Red faced he sat back down.

'My turn.' He flicked the bottle round. You could almost hear him willing it to land on Hannah. It didn't. It landed on Lizzie instead. She picked truth and was asked what's the worst lie she's ever told. She then started on some really boring story about how she lost her Mum's wedding ring and told everyone her baby brother swallowed it. An emergency trip to casualty followed, but the mystery of the ring was never solved. Until now. Dullsville or what? It would have been better if the kid had swallowed the ring.

More dares followed. Snagger had to drag on a joint. I don't even think it was real. It smelt like ordinary tobacco to me, but Snagger made a big thing of it. Then he took the bottle and spun it round. I watched it whizz round and stop at Sarah. She went very pale and stared at it in horror. Snagger glanced at Beaky and they both grinned.

'Truth or Dare?' Snagger asked her.

Sarah looked at me. I shrugged. It was up to her to choose.

'Dare?' She said it so quietly Snagger didn't hear her.

'What?'

'Dare.'

An evil glint lit up in Snagger's eyes. I knew he had something big planned for her.

Hannah

I really didn't want to go to the stupid party. I liked sleeping. Sleeping was good. I needed my sleep, otherwise I got the biggest bags under my eyes this side of a Tesco checkout till and was really grumpy. I knew Sarah felt the same, but we'd all just made up with Nancy and she wasn't going to take no for an answer.

After a few plastic cups of sour-tasting red wine (no idea where that had come from, probably nicked from the barbecue) I started to feel a bit better. And by the time someone suggested a game of truth or dare I was too giggly to think what a bad idea it probably was. I still gave Nancy the evils, though, just to let her know that she was still in the bad books and if she let Beaky anywhere near me I'd kill her.

I kept praying that the bottle would not stop at me and fate was with me, but not with Sarah. Snagger sent the bottle spinning and when it stopped it was facing her.

If it had been me I'd have wanted to leg it out of the room. I mean, how do you choose between truth without knowing what the question will be or dare not knowing what the dare will be? Impossible.

'Dare.' She said coolly, staring a challenge at Snagger. He looked at Beaky and seemed to be thinking really hard. Eventually he smiled.

'I dare you to kiss a girl. On the lips.'

My mouth dropped open and I looked at Sarah. She looked as horrified as I felt.

'I've changed my mind. Truth.'

'Too late. You've said dare now. You've got to do it. Them's the rulez. Isn't that right?' Snagger said, and everyone sitting in the circle nodded.

'I don't care. I'm not doing it.'

'It's not even a fair to ask her,' I added.

'I had to stick my bum out of the window,' Beaky mumbled. I gave him the filthiest of looks and I thought he was going to burst into tears.

'You can kiss me. I don't mind,' Nancy said. I think she thought she was being helpful, but really she should have been sticking up for Sarah. It was her stupid idea to join in the game in the first place.

'I'm not doing it.' Sarah stood up.

'Chicken,' Lizzie said, and Snagger started doing chicken impressions. Sarah started to go red.

'Come on, Sarah. It's just part of the game. No big deal.' Nancy was laughing.

I didn't see it coming, but suddenly Sarah

flipped. She turned on Nancy, waving an accusing finger at her.

'Nothing's a big deal to you, is it? Well, it is to me. You think you can tell us all what to do, and if we don't agree there's something wrong with us. What makes you so much better than us? I'll tell you what . . . nothing. You're not better. You don't know more than we do. All you are is . . . is a bitchy, loud-mouthed bully who likes making people feel like the dirt on the bottom of your shoes.'

Sarah stormed out of the room, knocking over empty bottles and cans as she went, leaving all of us in shock. I'd never seen her lose her temper before. Even Nancy looked stunned. After a few moments she got up and left the room. The rest of us looked at each other, not quite sure what to say. The party petered out soon after that, and I walked back to the room. Sarah and Nancy were already in bed. I got under the duvet totally fed up. We were right back where we started. Why couldn't they go for longer than a few hours without falling out?

Mud and Murphy

MONDAY

Nancy

I'd been having a nightmare. I was in the château, running from room to room and not one person would talk to me. There were all these stuffed animals on window ledges and stuck on walls and they were all alive and would say to me as I went past 'everyone hates you' and 'go home, no one wants you here' and other horrible stuff. Then suddenly Sarah was nudging my arm and asking me if I was awake. I looked at the time. It was half past six. Hannah was still fast asleep, curled up under her duvet.

'I'm really sorry about last night. At the party. I didn't mean those things I said. I'd had too much to drink and I kind of lost it.'

'Kind of? We were just having a laugh.'

'I know. I'm sorry. I guess alcohol and me don't really mix.'

'Do you really think I'm a bully?'

'No, of course not.' She smiled, but somehow I didn't believe her, 'Do you forgive me?'

'Of course.' I smiled back. She seemed happy with that, and disappeared out of the room, heading for the swimming pool. So much for her 'I'm not training' vow.

I closed my eyes and tried to go back to sleep, but I couldn't get the image of Sarah calling me a bully out of my head. Is that what she really thought about me? She could take it back all she wanted and blame it on the drink, but don't they say people's true feelings come out when they're drunk? I'd never thought of myself as a bully but maybe bullies never do. I didn't want to be one. Bullies were horrible. Bullies were people like Stacy. I wasn't like her, was I?

It made me even more determined to fix her up with Murphy, show her that I wasn't as bad as she thought. A real bully wouldn't do anything so nice for their friends. A bully would try and get the guy for herself. If I did a completely selfless act, that would prove to everyone I wasn't a bully.

I couldn't wait for the clock to tick round to breakfast time. I had a strategy to put into action.

Murphy was the perfect person to get Sarah's mind off Rhys and for me to prove myself as a good person. If Sarah fell for Murphy, Hannah would never have to find out what had been going on and we would all stay friends. It was all dead simple. As I was getting ready for breakfast I told Hannah that I was going to get Sarah and Murphy together. She seemed surprised but once she'd got over that she was really pleased. She told me that she was sure Sarah did like him, at least a little bit. What wasn't to like, she said . . . he was the Cockney twin of Seth Cohen after all? I don't watch bubble-headed crap like the OC, but she was right. He *was* quite cute, from a distance, and, really, did it matter if Sarah fancied him? Murphy fancied her, and I was sure if he was persistent enough she'd give in eventually and go out with him. At least it would show her there were other boys in the world apart from you know who. OK, there was the small problem of Schizoid Stacy, but I could sort her out. So that was the plan. Get Sarah and Murphy together. Step one was to find out which activities he'd signed up for. Step two was to sign us up for the same activities. Step three was to get them talking. Step four . . . I hoped step four would take care of itself.

'Anyone sitting here?' I didn't wait for an answer. I put my tray on the table and sat down opposite Murphy and his mates. Schizoid woman was nowhere in sight.

Murphy looked at me closely.

'You're Sarah's mate, aren't you?'

His two Neanderthal buddies grinned and grunted. They looked like a hideously deformed version of Ant and Dec.

'Best mate. We do everything together.'

'Apart from eat breakfast.' He smirked.

Smart arse.

'What's your name?' he asked, still looking at me.

'Nancy. What's yours?'

'Murphy.'

'I mean your real name.'

'Murphy is my real name. Murphy Jones. At your service.' He exchanged grins with Ant and Dec. He was pretty sure of himself. 'And these two weirdos are Gordy and Nick. I keep trying to shake 'em off, but they keep coming back insisting that they're my mates.'

'Maybe if you stopped paying them.'

He laughed. The longer I looked at him the more like Seth Cohen he became.

'But then I'd get all lonely.' He pulled this hangdog expression. I wasn't about to fall for that.

'Where you from anyway?'

'Walthamstow. I feel like I'm on a quiz show. My hobbies are football and girls, my favourite colour is red and I like singing in the shower. What's the prize if I win?'

'What prize would you like?'

'That would be telling.'

He grinned at me. I found myself grinning back. This wasn't quite going as planned. What was I supposed to be doing again? Oh yeah . . .

'What d'you think of this place so far?' Now I was sounding like a panto audience member. Really cool, Nancy.

'The scenery's nice.' He looked straight at me. If I didn't know any better I'd think he was flirting with me. I felt myself go red.

'So, erm . . . you decided what you're doing today?' God, that sounded lame. I was supposed to be doing this all MI5-like. It didn't help when Ant and Dec started sniggering into their cereal. I went even redder. I hoped their cornflakes choked them.

'Quad bikes this morning, then potholing this afternoon. I'm going to try and cure my fear of enclosed spaces. I might need someone to hold my hand.'

Before I could answer Hannah appeared next to me.

'Morning.' She sat down, giving me a very approving look. 'Hi, I'm Hannah.'

'Nice to meet you, Hannah. I'm Murphy.'

'I know. Sarah mentioned you.' Subtle as a scud missile is Hannah. I kicked her on the ankle. She yelped and gave me a dirty look.

'She did?'

'Only because it was your fault she nearly got battered last night.' I saved the situation. 'If that psycho comes near us again . . .'

'You mean Stacy? I'll tell her to stay well clear. She's a bit possessive, that's all. We went out for like a day or something in year nine. I guess I just have this weird effect on women . . . they can't forget me.'

'You turn them into homicidal freaks? Nice.'

He pulled a face at me.

'I'd love to stay here all day and have you insult me but I'm not sure my fragile male ego can stand it.' He got up. Ant and Dec copied him. He looked at me and smiled as he picked up his tray. 'You going into the village tonight? There are a couple of bars. It's supposed to be OK. You can insult me some more if you like.'

My mind went blank again.

'We'll see you there.' Hannah stepped in. I hoped she hadn't noticed me getting all tongue-tied.

'Cool.' He started to walk away. He stopped and turned back for a moment, 'Will you say hi to Sarah for me and tell her I'm sorry about Stacy hassling her. Oh, and tell her she really should come down for breakfast. It's the most important meal of the day.'

As soon as he was out of earshot Hannah started babbling with excitement.

'Oh, my God. He so fancies Sarah. Did you hear him? Say hi to Sarah for me . . . He is totally into her. Come on, let's go back up and tell her.'

For a moment I wished that Hannah had got it wrong, that he wasn't interested in Sarah. But then I remembered what we'd vowed last night – to stick together and never let boys come between us. Murphy was the perfect person to make sure that vow was kept. I got up, my resolve restored. 'Operation Sarah & Murphy' (Surphy?) was back on and we had a morning of quad biking to get ready for.

'What are you waiting for?' I asked. Hannah grinned, and we headed for our room.

I don't know why I was bothered anyway. He wasn't *all that*. Not really.

Hannah

'Oh . . . my . . . God.' I stood and looked at the quad bikes lined up in front of us. 'If you think I'm getting on one of those things you're a mentalist.'

It wasn't just the quad bikes that were putting me off, though they were a huge part of it – noisy, smelly, fast and dangerous. I mean, in what possible way could charging round on one of them be described as fun? But there were other factors putting me off too – the track marked out by straw bales in the muddiest looking field, disappearing into the spookiest looking woods this side of anywhere, and the unflattering jumpsuit things we were supposed to wear – puke yellow with pervy black rubber elbow and knee pads – to name just two. But worst of all were the horrific helmets. If I put one of those on I'd look like something off Wallace and Gromit. No way was I wearing any of that stuff. No way was I getting on one of those machines and no way was I going anywhere near that field, with that mud and the possibility of crashing and dying in a ball of flames or, even worse, not being able to get the stupid bike thing moving, crawling round at two miles an hour and being laughed at by everyone. Not a chance.

I fixed Nancy with what I hoped was a 'don't even try to argue with me' expression. But this was Nancy we were talking about. Everything was a potential argument.

'What you moaning about?'

Sarah was already pulling on her jumpsuit.

There was this glint in her eye. I guess the same glint you get in the eye of a Grand Prix driver about to race around Brands Hatch.

'There are loads of activities we could have done this morning. There was a trip to a chocolate factory.'

'What, are you Willy Wonka's long lost great-great-granddaughter or something?' The expression on her face made the words die in my mouth. She could make you feel the size of a pea by just raising an eyebrow.

'We're here because Murphy is here.'

She looked over to where Murphy and his mates – who Nancy had christened Ant and Dec and the names had stuck – were strapping on their Wallace and Gromit helmets and pretending to listen to the instructor as he explained how everything worked. Murphy looked over at Sarah and then at Nancy and me. He didn't do anything so geeky as wave, but he did grin and wink. Winking to me is a huge turn off. Creepy guys wink. Sleazebuckets wink. Winking in any form is a bad thing, even if the person winking looks like Murphy. He's not quite right, I thought to myself. Not to be trusted.

'Don't you want to get him and Sarah together?'

I'd thought it was a good idea until the wink.

Now I wasn't so sure. I was just about to say as much when Sarah appeared next to me.

'What are you talking about?' Sarah was now wearing the jumpsuit. It looked OK on her, but Sarah could wear a bin bag and still look really pretty. I'd just look like a small banana as soon as I put mine on.

'Nothing.' Nancy gave me a little sideways smirk before turning back to Sarah, 'You ever ridden one of these things before?'

'No. It can't be that hard, though. What about you?'

'One of my friends at my old school had a farm and we used to borrow her brother's.'

Great. So Nancy already knew how to work one and Sarah was so competitive she'd soon get the hang of it. Then there was me. It had taken me years to learn how to ride a bike. Even Josh got rid of his stabilizers before I did and I'm nearly two years older than him. I knew I'd be rubbish at quad biking. The only silver lining in the big black cloud was that Sarah and Nancy seemed to have forgotten about the night before. I didn't know who had said sorry to who and I didn't want to ask in case it set them off again. They were friends and that was enough. It still didn't quite make up for having to wear the stupid yellow suits.

Nancy picked up the jumpsuit. At least she looked a little unsure about it, which made me feel slightly better.

'I guess you won't see the putrid colour once we're covered in mud.' She nodded at me trying to encourage me, I guess. It didn't work. If I wanted to get covered in mud I'd go to a health spa and have one of those mud wrap things. At least there's a point to that – you get nice soft skin and a healthy glow.

'I think I'll just watch.' I was about to head a safe distance away when the instructor came over to us.

He was about twenty-eight, I guessed, and he was almost the spitting image of Freddie Prinze Jr, but from *She's All That*, not the Scooby-Doo movies because they were crap.

He smiled at me, like he could sense my fear.

'Great to see some girls here. I always wish more girls would be brave enough to have a go on the quads.' He had a strange accent, German or maybe Swedish. Wherever he was from he sounded really cute. 'I'm Conrad by the way. What are your names?'

'Nancy.' Nancy beamed at him, also recognizing the cute factor.

'Sarah.' She was already putting on her helmet.

'And you? The one who looks a little unsure?'

How did he know?

'Hannah.'

I was about to be annoyed at him, but he looked straight into my eyes.

'Well, Hannah, don't worry about a thing. I'll look after you.'

Nancy nudged my arm and grinned.

'If you're lucky,' she whispered under her breath. I went red, certain he'd heard her.

Conrad demonstrated how the quad bikes worked. It even sounded simple the way he explained it. One hand made it go faster, the other hand controlled the brakes. He told us to take it slow at first – he looked at me when he said it, which didn't seem fair – and not to cut people up when they wanted to overtake. Anyone driving dangerously would be disqualified and removed from the track. I'd probably be removed from the track for going too slowly and holding everyone else up. How embarrassing would that be?

Murphy and his mates were already lining up at the start along with a few other victims. Sarah and Nancy roared over to join them. I hadn't even got the hang of starting the thing.

'Take your time. No rush. It isn't a race,' Conrad told me.

Yeah, try telling that to everyone else. Sarah was revving her engine like a woman possessed.

Murphy started revving his, trying to outdo her. They did seem suited for each other. Nancy had better be right. If I had to endure this something good had better come out of it. Maybe I would have an accident and Conrad would run over to my stricken body, full of remorse, and give me the kiss of life?

I got my quad bike started and, after stalling it twice on the way over, I finally caught up with the others.

'All right?' Nancy asked.

'No.' I glared at her. Ant and Dec looked over at me and started laughing before revving their engines and wheel-spinning off down the track spraying mud and cack everywhere. A big dollop landed on the top of my helmet and dripped on to the end of my nose. Nancy and Sarah stared at me, mouths open, and started giggling.

'Come on, girls. Let's see what you're made of.' Murphy grinned, his eyes fastened on Sarah. She went red. He sped off down the field. She shrugged at us and disappeared after him.

'You'll be OK,' Nancy decided, and she went too, leaving me all alone, all alone apart from Conrad, who I swear was laughing at me. Why am I the punch line to everyone's jokes? God, I hate my life sometimes.

*

An hour and a half later and it was all over. The only part of me not covered in mud was my eyelids. Every part of me ached and I was sure I'd be covered in bruises for weeks. I'd lost count of the number of times I'd stalled the bike and been lapped by the others. My humiliation was complete when I got stuck in the middle of a big ditch and every single person flew past spraying me with stuff that smelt like it had come out of the back end of a cow. Sarah didn't even seem to notice I was in trouble; she was so dead set on being the fastest. The only person who stopped was Nancy. She helped me drag the bike out of the ditch, but we couldn't get it to start. So she stayed with me as I pushed it back to the start. I think she felt bad for the whole thing because she said I could choose what we did that afternoon, and it didn't have to be anything that Murphy was doing.

Apart from Nancy being really sweet, this had been the worst day of my life. Well, not quite, but it was up there, just below the day that Sarah was first round at my house and met Rhys and realized that she'd been out on a date with my brother.

She hadn't known he was my brother, and he hadn't known she was my friend from school. He hadn't even known that she was still at school. She'd told him she was a student teacher or something. That was a really crappy day. This wasn't anywhere near as bad as that. Nothing was anywhere near as bad as that. I thought I'd lost Sarah as a friend.

It was hard enough to believe she could fancy my brother in the first place – that anyone could fancy him was well weird. I mean, he's scruffy and never combs his hair, and he listens to awful music that's just noise and screaming and don't even start me on his best mate Gilly – complete Neanderthals both of them. But for some reason she did. Before we both knew it was my brother she was talking about, she would tell me about him and it was like she was in love. They even had nicknames for each other. She called him Animal and he called her Hustler. So neither knew the other's real name.

But after that day where they came face to face with each other in my kitchen – it makes me cringe just to think of it now and it was months ago, well before Christmas – I'd automatically expected her to back off. You just don't go out with your friends' brothers. Even after she'd promised she wasn't interested any more she still accidentally on purpose bumped into him at his college. I know he got fed up of it. He even told me she wasn't allowed round at our house. There was lots of shouting and yelling – which I hate – but in the end Sarah admitted she had been interested, but Rhys obviously wasn't and that she would forget all about him. Since then we've done everything together . . . well, apart from when she's at swim training or the gym, or at one of her Pilates classes that she does to help her breathing or something. She's my best friend. Nicole and Nancy are, too, but Sarah is the first one I think of texting or phoning when I have some gossip to spill. I'm sure we'll still be friends when we're both married with kids. We've already agreed to be each other's bridesmaids. All we both have to do is find ourselves a groom each.

Sarah

Hannah was in the shower. She'd been in there for what felt like an hour but she had got really muddy. I don't think she enjoyed the quad biking at all. I thought it was fun. It was nice to compete at something and not have to worry about getting my stroke just right, or my breathing or my tumble turns, or think what Mum would say if I came second not first. I felt really free just whizzing along on the bike with the wind against my face.

For the whole time we were racing I didn't think about Rhys or swimming once.

Now I was back in the room I couldn't think about anything else. I'd finished drying my hair and was looking at myself in the mirror. How old *did* I look? Without any make-up I did look really young. Maybe if I cut my hair really short or into a bob I'd look older? If only I could go to sleep and when I woke up two years would have gone by and Rhys would be mine.

'So?' Nancy crashed on to the bed behind me. I went red, as if she could read my thoughts.

'So what?'

'What do you think of Murphy?' By the smile on her face I knew she was plotting something.

'He's OK.' He was OK. It had been fun racing him on the quad bikes, though I knew he'd let me win, which was kind of patronizing. I would have beaten him anyway.

'Just OK? Or more than OK? How do you rate him – on a scale of one to ten?'

'I don't know. I hadn't thought.'

'Well, think now.'

I did as I was told and put on my best thinking face.

'Six?' I offered.

'Six?' She pulled a face, 'He's so much better than a six.'

'Seven, then.' I paused. 'And a half.'

She seemed happy with that.

'But I don't fancy him.'

She looked at me in disbelief.

'Why not? You just scored him a seven and a half. If you score anyone over a six that must mean you fancy them.'

'Does it?'

She narrowed her eyes.

'What does Rhys score?'

I felt myself flush.

'I thought we said we weren't going to talk about him?'

'Fine by me. Let's talk about Murphy instead. He really fancies you.'

'No he doesn't,' But a little part of me was quite pleased. 'How do you know?'

'I was talking to him at breakfast.'

'And he said he fancied me?'

'Not exactly. But he asked about you. And I could tell this morning. He kept looking at you. When a lad keeps looking over at you that's a big sign.'

'Oh.' All I could think of was whether Rhys would be jealous if he knew.

'So would you go out with him if he asked you?'

'Nah.'

'Why not? I thought you wanted a boyfriend.

You're always complaining that your Mum won't let you have one. This is the perfect opportunity. And you just admitted you fancied him.'

'No I didn't.'

'Whatever. I don't understand you. Here's this fit lad who really likes you, and you like him, even if you won't admit it. What's to stop you going out on one date?'

'He hasn't even asked me yet.' I was stalling. Nancy knew I was stalling.

'But if he does?'

I didn't say anything.

'The only reason I can think you would turn him down is if you're interested in someone else.' She was eyeing me in the mirror, waiting for my reaction.

'I'm not.'

'So go out with Murphy then. You might even enjoy yourself. There is life after Rhys you know.'

'I haven't even had a life with Rhys.' I turned to face her and couldn't keep the anger out of my voice.

She looked at me.

'And you never will. So going out with Murphy would be the first step in your . . .' she thought hard . . . 'rehabilitation. RA. Rhys Anonymous, like Alcoholics Anonymous, only without the group therapy bit.'

Hannah chose that exact moment to crash through the door.

'I thought I'd never get the mud out of my hair.' She sat down on the bed next to Nancy. 'What are we talking about?'

Nancy gave me a look, then smiled at Hannah.

'We were talking about Murphy.'

Hannah grinned at me.

'Do you fancy him? He's really into you. I think you'd be perfect together.'

I sighed and turned back to the mirror. Nancy was right. I should try and go out with other boys but in the end what was the point when I was in love with someone else and those feelings would never change?

Nancy

After the quad biking there was no way I could persuade Hannah to go potholing with the lads. I wasn't that keen myself to be honest. I'd watched the film Descent with Jake when Becca was out one night and, after seeing that, no one in their right mind would want to wander about in caves. I had nightmares for weeks afterwards and Becca had a go at Jake because of it. Becca won't watch horror movies, but Jake's a bit of an uber-fan on the quiet. In fact he's a lot nicer than

I thought he was. I know I hadn't wanted Becca to marry him, once a cheater always a cheater and all that, but when he was being thoughtful and sensitive he wasn't actually too bad a person. I'd even go as far to say that he'd started to grow on me. And not like some horrible carbuncle-type growth, either.

When my Dad had his heart attack, Jake really took charge. Becca and me were a mess, but he was Mr Practical and organized everything. I used to think being 'Mr Practical' made him 'Mr Dull', but when bad things happened, like with my Dad, you needed someone who's practical to take over.

Maybe Becca had been right to marry him after all? Though she'd been so moody lately I was worried that she was beginning to think the exact opposite. I don't suppose it helped with me being around and getting in the way all the time. Sometimes I felt like a spare part. But at least me being away in France would give them some space.

One thing was for sure – I was never going to get married. Not until I was at least thirty anyway.

I was going to enjoy myself first and have loads of different boyfriends.

That was the theory anyway.

The reality was that my romantic life had been a wasteland lately.

In fact since I'd been living in Hollyoaks there hadn't really been anyone. I'd had a pash with Justin at New Year, but that just ended up with me falling out with the girls.

And he wasn't that great a kisser.

Well, actually, he was an amazing kisser, but when you looked at him, really looked at him, his legs were kind of stumpy and he had no sense of humour at all. He took everything so seriously. Sixteen going on sixty. I knew I was well out of it. We might all prefer older lads now, but not ones with the mental age of a pensioner.

But my new selfless self was putting my own love life on hold for a while. Sarah was the priority.

Sarah

The plan that night was to go into the village and check out the 'local talent' – Nancy's words, not mine. Murphy was going to be there according to her. It would be better for everyone if Murphy could be like a big magic wand. One wave from him and I would forget all my feelings for Rhys and fancy him instead. I would be happy, Nancy would approve and there'd be no secrets from Hannah. Life would be simple.

But life wasn't simple. Even if it seemed like my two friends had already planned my destiny with Murphy. If it were up to them we'd be together by the end of the week. What I wanted seemed to have nothing to do with anything.

The fact was I felt dead guilty that I'd even considered that going out with Murphy would solve all my problems. Guilty even though it had only ever been a very distant and completely unlikely happening, and that I'd only thought about the possibility for the sum total of five seconds. Did thinking about someone else count as cheating? But how could it be cheating? In order to cheat on someone you have to be going out with them, don't you? In anyone else's life that would have been the case. But not in my mess of a life. I still felt like I'd betrayed Rhys.

It didn't help one bit when Hannah put on her James Blunt CD. She loved James Blunt. She loved his CD so much she'd worn out her original copy. I loved that CD, too, but his songs made me cry because they reminded me of Rhys. I know that's pathetic, but I can't help it.

Every couple has a song. It's just in normal relationships the song means something to you both. But 'High' was my Rhys song. He hated it. He did this really funny impression of Mr Blunt that made me laugh, but also made me love the song even more at the same time. But that was then, before it all went wrong. And now whenever I hear that song I want to cry.

Even though the Rhys I know now is nice to me and treats me as a friend, the song still reminds me totally and utterly of the Rhys who went from loving me (wishful thinking) to ignoring me. It takes me right back to that horrible, horrible day at Hannah's and he was there in the kitchen and he'd looked at me standing there in my school uniform as if I was something repulsive he'd scraped off the bottom of his Converses.

All day at school I'd been so happy reliving our date, the way he looked at me, the way his eyes didn't just look at me but looked right into me. The way he took hold of my hand. The way he kissed me – the most amazing kiss ever – and the way he was so happy afterwards, like he wanted to run down the street yelling. I'd never felt so alive than at that moment. I'd gone home with the biggest smile plastered all over my face. For the first time I knew what being in love was like and I'd put on James Blunt and played 'High' on repeat and thought how amazing it was that my life was suddenly so perfect.

Then the day after, round at Hannah's, there he was, and it turns out he's her brother and my little white fib about being the same age as him – which wasn't really a fib at all, more of a not saying anything – comes crashing down around me.

I went from being the happiest I've ever been to wanting to shrivel up and die. I so badly wanted him to look at me like he had on our date. So after that day whenever I listened to James Blunt I cried because it reminded me of how my happiness had turned into never-ending misery.

So there was no way I could listen to that CD at the same time as pretending to be excited at getting ready for a night out. At first I suggested we put something else on. Hannah started rifling through the CDs I'd brought and held up the Arcade Fire one that Rhys had given to me. She pulled a weird face and said 'Rhys has this. I didn't know you were into them?'

I froze. It was a horrible moment. I couldn't think what to say.

But Nancy saved me. She said it was one of hers (because she's more likely to listen to that sort of 'alternative weird stuff that no one's ever heard of' than me) and had got mixed up with mine by mistake. Hannah seemed happy with the explanation but ended up putting James Blunt on anyway.

Instead I got ready really quick – because I wasn't that bothered what I looked like – and went down to the computer room to email Rhys. We emailed each other quite a lot. His emails were usually three lines of nothing or some bad jokes – which he always blamed on Gilly. But however bad the joke it always made me laugh because Rhys had sent it to me.

I logged into my account hoping that there'd be an email from him waiting for me. I wanted it so much I even closed my eyes as the screen came up and then opened them a squint at a time as if that would summon it up. It didn't work. No email from Rhys.

There was just junk – what did I need Viagra for anyway? – a very short email from Mum reminding me about training, which I deleted without reading, and a long one from Dad hoping I was having a nice time and complaining about Mum nagging him and Amy suddenly wanting a cat. Amy being Amy, the cat she wanted wasn't just any old moggie but something called a Bengal Leopard cat, which would cost at least £500. My little sister had no idea about anything.

I told myself that Rhys was probably too busy studying or out with Gilly to email me or maybe he didn't think I'd be checking my email account so soon and had thought there was no point sending anything yet. Or maybe he was waiting for me to email him first. Maybe he thought I was too busy to email him. Too busy thinking about other boys. Like Murphy. Too busy wondering what it would be like if I could fancy someone other than him. But he wouldn't be thinking that. He probably wasn't thinking about me at all. I could make him think about me, though.

I started to type. I got as far as 'Hi, Rhys' and then couldn't think of anything else to say. I didn't want to sound like I was enjoying myself, but I didn't want to sound like I wasn't. Part of me wanted to mention Murphy, tell him that someone else was interested in me, but then another part of me was afraid of the reply I might get back – 'that's fantastic, I hope you'll be very happy together'. I'd die if he said that. What I'd want would be for him to read about Murphy, jump in his car and drive all the way to France to sweep me off my feet and declare his undying love.

I shook myself. I was starting to sound like Hannah. Not in a million years did that sort of thing happen. Only in Hollywood movies. And Hannah's imagination.

So what could I write to him about? Boys like it when you act interested in them and ask them what they're doing. I read that in one of Hannah's magazines. I started to ask about what he'd been doing so far this week when I heard the door open behind me. Some instinct or other made me hit delete and the email disappeared. I turned round to see Hannah poking her head around the door. I could feel myself turning red. That was far too close.

'We're ready to go,' She stepped further into the room, 'Who you emailing?'

'No one', I said quickly. 'Just checking what people have sent me.'

She peered over my shoulder.

'Your Mum and your Dad?' She pulled a face. 'I don't think either of my 'rents even know how to turn a computer on.'

'I kind of wish mine didn't either.' I shrugged and logged out. 'Come on, let's get going.'

'Yeah . . . you don't want to keep Murphy waiting.' She beamed at me. I had a sinking feeling I was heading somewhere I didn't want to go.

'You won't . . . erm . . . leave me with him . . . or try and set me up, will you?'

She looked thoughtful for a moment.

'Not if you don't want me to.' She narrowed her eyes. 'But if you change your mind we should have a signal. If he comes over and you're getting along and you want us to go you should nod your head, or maybe say something like "I loved Orlando Bloom's last film".'

'What?'

'Well, if you say that, we'll know what you mean but he'll be clueless. So he doesn't know you weren't sure about him.'

'Can us three not just stick together? It's you two I came on holiday with.'

'Don't worry about us, we don't mind if you pull. Honest. We won't feel left out as long as you tell us all about it after.' She linked her arm in mine and led me to the door. I let myself follow. How guilty did I feel? She's such a good person, wanting me to be happy, and there I was thinking all those thoughts about her brother, about to email him, all behind her back. Is that what being in love did to you?

Hannah

'Where should we go?' Sarah asked as we stood in the little square at the centre of the village. There were five cafes and three bars on the square, plus lots of narrow streets disappearing off into the distance that promised even more places to eat and drink.

The village was just as you'd imagine a French village to be. Cute old buildings with pointed roofs that looked hundreds of years old, cobbled roads, lots of trees and, of course, all the cafes, restaurants and bars with chairs and tables outside.

Some of the cafes were home to the crinkled-up old residents of the village. A couple of the men even wore berets, which seemed to really please Nancy. They sat and watched us walk by like we were the evening entertainment. Nancy waved at a couple of them. They raised their bushy eyebrows and muttered something in French to each other, which wasn't very friendly. I mean, they must be used to being invaded by British teenagers by now, but they definitely weren't about to welcome us with open arms and invite us home for croissants and coffee. We kept walking to avoid those places and that's why we ended up in the square.

'Where did Murphy say he was going?' I looked at Nancy.

'He didn't. Not specifically.' She looked a little embarrassed. 'I didn't think there'd be a choice of places to go.'

'I think that one looks nice.' Sarah sounded relieved. Maybe she'd been worried in case Nancy had set it up so we'd go into a café, see him waiting there on his own and we'd then make excuses and disappear. If nothing happened with him tonight I was sure that would be Nancy's next move. I'd have to talk her out of it. Sarah wouldn't be happy and I didn't want them to fall out again.

Sarah led us over to a café called Le Café des Amis, which even I could translate as meaning the Café of Friends. It seemed fitting and a couple of girls we recognized from the château were sitting at one of the tables outside. They were from the same school as Stacy and they gave us the bitchiest of looks as we walked up.

'Maybe we should go somewhere else.' Sarah slowed down.

'Why should we?' Nancy linked her arm and dragged her inside.

It was a good choice. I felt happy as soon as we walked in the door. The Kaiser Chiefs were playing on the ginormous fifties jukebox. A crowd of boys from our school were standing next to it. I spotted Beaky straight away, but as he towered over everyone else it was impossible to miss him. He looked over and smiled at me. I averted my eyes quickly.

'He's going red, bless him.' Nancy had seen him too. 'He lurves you so much.'

'He better not come over,' I said as we commandeered a table at the window.

'This is Beaky we're talking about.' Sarah giggled.

'He'd never dare speak to you,' Nancy joined in. 'His head would explode before he'd said one word. And if you actually said something to him . . .'

'He'd die on the spot,' Sarah added.

'But at least he'd die happy.' Nancy waved over at him. He went even redder and dropped all the coins he was holding. His mates started laughing as he scrabbled on the floor to find his money, which made Nancy and Sarah giggle.

'Freaky Beaky,' Nancy said, between giggles.

I smiled along with them, but felt a bit bad for doing it. Poor Beaky. He was terrified of girls. If he did speak to one of us it was only because it was in class and he had no other choice. Even then he struggled to get whole sentences out. Instead he spoke in single words, getting redder and redder by the second.

I knew he fancied me because he'd told his mates, who'd told Nancy, who told me. Even if it hadn't got back to me, it was pretty obvious. I was always catching him looking at me across a room or in the playground or the canteen with big puppy-dog eyes. There was no way on this planet I would ever even think about going out with him, but I did feel sorry for him. Boys are expected to be dead cool and confident with girls, but most of them – the ones our age anyway – don't have a clue. The only thing they can talk about in full sentences is football – penalties this, referee that, what should have been a goal and what shouldn't. Extreme boredom or what?

No wonder we've all decided we're only interested in boys who are at least a year older than us – meaning minimum seventeen and not in our year. Boys that age can actually string sentences together about things that matter – global warming, healthy eating, the latest movies and the best places to go on holiday (money no object). And when older guys talk to you they actually sound like they're interested in what you're saying. The boys in our year have the concentration span of a brain-damaged goldfish.

We ordered pancakes (*crêpes*) and a bottle of white wine. Nancy chose which one as she said her Dad was a bit of a wine buff and it was one that he liked to drink.

'I like France,' Sarah said as she took a sip of wine.

'Just because you're allowed to drink?' Nancy nudged me, 'We'll have to watch this one. She'll be an alcy by Friday.'

'No. I just mean it's more relaxed. You don't have to sneak around or worry about not being served and getting kicked out. And after last night

I'm never getting drunk again.' Her and Nancy smiled at each other.

'It's good not to be treated like a kid all the time.' I nodded. I didn't normally like wine, but the stuff Nancy had chosen tasted quite nice. A couple of sips and I could already feel it rushing up to meet my brain.

'To France.' Nancy held up her glass. Sarah and I held up our own glasses and we chinked them across the middle of the table.

'To France.'

'And being able to do whatever we like.'

We all chinked again.

'Whenever we feel like it.'

Chink.

'With whoever we want.'

Chink. Nancy gave Sarah a strange look, so strange that I looked round to see if Murphy had come in. He was nowhere in sight. I turned back to Nancy to say something when she prodded my arm. Really hard.

'Oh, my God.' She was looking past me. I turned, and suddenly Beaky was there, hovering right in front of our table. He didn't say anything, just stared down at me and tangled his fingers together.

'I didn't know you worked here. Fast work that. We only arrived yesterday.' Nancy grinned at

Sarah and me. 'Can we see the dessert menu?'

'I . . . erm . . .' He blushed and mumbled, 'I just came over to . . . erm . . .'

He seemed to forget what he was going to say next.

I could see his mates watching from the other side of the room. They were killing themselves laughing. I gave them the daggers and they shut up.

'There's . . . erm . . . a footie match on TV later . . . we're, erm . . . all going to one of the bars to watch it . . .'

'How nice for you.' Nancy rolled her eyes. 'Football's for losers.'

He looked shocked.

'But . . . you . . . Justin . . . he loves footie . . . I thought you . . . and him . . .'

'Go on. Spit it out.' She gave him her iciest stare.

'Did you . . . weren't you . . . ? Is that why he's not here?'

'Justin's a little kid. I wouldn't touch him with yours. And I'd have to be dead to touch yours in the first place. At the very least I'd have to have my arm amputated.'

She took a big gulp of wine and we all sat in silence for a moment. The subject of Justin is a very touchy one as far as Nancy is concerned.

They had a thing at New Year, but I don't think he was really that interested. She claims she's so over him now, but she says it with too much feeling for someone who doesn't care.

She was definitely disappointed when we found out he wasn't coming to France. His excuse was that, as he'd already lost so much time, when he'd had all that trouble with the police last year, he needed to stay behind and study. Maybe there was truth in that, but I think it was more because he didn't see himself as one of us lot. He was different to the other boys in our year, but then anyone who's been in prison, even just for a few weeks, isn't going to come out and be the same person they were before. But it's sad that he doesn't seem interested in even being friends with any of us. And him and Nancy would make a nice couple. He's a bit mean and moody for me but that makes him Nancy's ideal man. If it's meant to be they'll end up together. That's one of my little rules of life and love.

Beaky and me – that's one relationship never ever meant to be.

He seemed to have glued himself to the floor by our table. He wasn't giving up easily.

'Me and . . . erm . . . me mates . . . erm . . . wondered if you . . . any of you wanted . . . erm . . . anything on the . . . erm . . . jukebox.'

'Are you still talking?' Nancy spat out the words. I could tell she was brooding about Justin, but it wasn't right to take it out on Beaky. It wasn't his fault. I kicked her on the ankle. She yelped and glared at me.

'We're OK, thanks, Beaky.' I smiled at him. 'It was nice of you to ask.'

He looked at me like I'd just agreed to marry him or something. His mouth twisted into a goofy grin.

'If you change your mind.'

'I'm pretty sure we won't.' Nancy kicked me back and it didn't take long for me to realize why. Now I'd encouraged him he would never leave us alone.

'So, erm . . . this place . . . pretty cool . . . isn't it?' His confidence was growing.

'I guess.' My heart started to sink. All I'd done was say eleven words to him and now he thought he was in with a chance? Why can't boys see the difference between friendly and flirty? To them they're the same thing, but to us they couldn't be further apart.

'What you, erm . . . doing tomorrow?'

My heart stopped beating. Was he asking me out? I could feel Sarah and Nancy staring at me. I felt their horror.

'I mean . . . what have you signed up for?'

Thank God.

'What have you signed up for?' Nancy stepped in.

He looked at her for a moment, suspecting a trick question.

'Archery.'

She pulled a face.

'We can cross that one off our list.'

A frown flickered across his face. He glanced at me as if he expected me to say something nice or leap to his defence. It just wasn't going to happen. When would he take the hint and go?

'See you then.' Nancy must have read my thoughts.

'What? Oh . . .' His eyes fixed on me. I could feel them even though I didn't look up, 'See you later . . . maybe . . .'

I didn't answer and he shuffled back to his mates. He wasn't even out of earshot when Nancy went off on one of her rants.

'See you later? Is he on drugs or something?'

'You don't need to shout it to the whole room.' All I wanted to do was forget the whole horrible experience.

'I think he must have drunk quite a lot.' Sarah picked up the wine bottle and refilled our glasses, 'He'd never have got the courage to come over otherwise.'

'But to think he might be in with an actual chance . . .' Nancy shook her head.

'He's not that bad.' Sarah smiled at me. No wonder she was sympathetic to Beaky. She understood what it was like to fancy someone and not be fancied back.

'You have him then,' I said.

'I'm not saying he's boyfriend material or anything but at least he's quite considerate, asking us if we wanted any songs on the jukebox. That was a nice thing to do.'

'He didn't do it to be nice. He did it because he wants to get in Hannah's knickers.'

'Nancy.' I punched her on the arm.

'I'm sorry, but it's true. All boys are the same.'

'No they're not.' Sarah snapped back.

'Like you've got so much experience with the opposite sex.' They glared at each other. Our night out was turning into one big argument.

'I'm going to get us another bottle of wine.' I got up and didn't wait for an answer.

There were a few people before me at the bar so I started to look around the room. It was much busier than when we'd gone in. Every table was taken and the people who couldn't find tables stood about chatting. Lots of people were smoking; the air was clogged with it. Why anyone would want to smell like a mouldy old ashtray is beyond me. It makes you stink and kills you at the same time. Nancy tried her first cigarette when she was thirteen, but she doesn't smoke now. At least not when I'm around, as she knows I don't approve. Secretly, I'm sure, she thinks it looks cool. Really cool when you're gasping for breath and your lungs are full of cancer. I realized I was staring at a girl with a cigarette in her mouth and she didn't look too happy about it. I yanked my gaze away, and that's when it happened.

The crowd parted and there stood the most gorgeous boy I'd seen in my entire life. He was everything I'd ever dreamed about – curly black hair, olive-coloured skin, deep brown eyes and incredible lips that just made me want to run over and kiss them. I couldn't believe he was real. Then, as I stared over at him, he turned his head and looked straight at me.

Our eyes locked together. It was like there was no one else in the room. I couldn't hear anything, I couldn't smell anything; we were locked in our own private world. Just him and me. No one else existed.

And then, slowly, playfully he smiled. His eyes smiled, his beautiful lips smiled, his whole face smiled.

At me. My stomach flipped over and didn't stop. My knees went so weak I thought I'd fall over. And then I smiled back. I couldn't help it. I had no control at all. My mouth took over. I smiled. He kept smiling. We were connected like no two people have ever been connected. And it hit me. This is what it must be like to see your soulmate for the first time. He must be my soulmate. This was the moment I'd been waiting my whole life for.

'You not been served yet? What on earth are you doing?' Nancy's voice sliced into my moment. 'We're dying of thirst over there.'

I glanced at her, hoping a look would be enough to shut her up.

'What?' She looked at me, clueless to the momentous occasion happening right before her eyes.

I looked back to where he was standing. But the crowd had merged into one big mess of people and I couldn't see him.

He was gone and I felt like someone had ripped out my heart.

Nancy

'What is it?' I asked Hannah again. She was staring at something on the other side of the room, bobbing her head from side to side like a demented pigeon.

'He's gone. He can't have. It's not fair. Come

on. I have GOT to find him.' She grabbed my arm and dragged me behind her as she pushed her way through the crowd. I was convinced she'd gone mental. She wasn't making any sense.

'Who are we looking for?'

'My soulmate. The man of my dreams. The person I'm supposed to spend the rest of my life with. The fittest, buffest boy ever to walk the planet.'

She had lost it.

'You were only gone five minutes.' How could anyone decide all that about another person in five minutes?

She skidded to a halt and rescanned the room.

'Five minutes or five seconds. It doesn't matter. Our eyes met and we both knew.'

She looked one way, then the other. Nothing. She set off again in a different direction. I had no choice but to follow her. I was seriously worried she needed professional help. Maybe the wine and smoke combination had altered her brain chemistry and turned her crazy.

'What did he say to you?'

'We didn't get chance to speak.'

I was about to point out that there was no way she could have met Mr Right without having actually met him, or without at least having made sure he didn't sound like the love child of David

Beckham and Bubble off *Ab Fab*, when she stopped again.

'There he is. Oh, my God. Look at him. He's amazing.'

I looked where she was looking but couldn't see anyone amazing.

'Which one?'

She looked at me as if I was the one going insane.

'Him. With the blue top and black hair.'

I looked again. There was a lad with a blue top and black hair, but he had a skinny face that made his nose look bigger than it was and half-moon eyebrows that gave him a permanently surprised expression. Apart from that he was OK. Even sort of cute I suppose, from the side, in a certain light, but amazing? Not really. Mr Right? Hardly. The guy Hannah's supposed to spend the rest of her life with? We're teenagers. Dating someone for six weeks is a life sentence.

'Isn't he the most gorgeous thing you've ever seen?'

I had to choose my answer carefully. We all saw different things in people. To Hannah he was the perfect male specimen, but to me he was just another guy, not repulsive or anything, but nothing special. I shouldn't be surprised really; she did have a strange taste in guys. She thought

Justin Timberlake was fanciable. The connection suddenly hit me. This guy and JT both had curly hair. Hannah had a curly hair fetish.

'He's not really my type,' I said in my most diplomatic voice. 'But he is cute.'

'Don't you just love his hair?'

I was right. It was the hair.

'What are you waiting for?'

'What d'you mean?' She couldn't take her eyes off him.

'Go over and talk to him.'

She looked at me as if I'd suggested taking off all her clothes and running round the café singing 'It's Raining Men'.

'I can't.'

'Why?'

'Because . . . because . . . I don't know. I just can't.'

'So how do you plan spending the rest of your life with him? Are you both going to learn sign language?'

'No . . . I . . . want to talk to him. But . . . but what if he doesn't like me?'

'You said your eyes met and you both knew?'

'He did smile the most amazing smile at me.'

'Of course he'll like you. What's not to like. Go on. Get over there. Look, he's on his own. It's the perfect opportunity.'

She stood rooted to the spot.

'It's too early.'

I looked at my watch.

'It's nearly ten-thirty. How much later do you need it to be?'

'No, I mean it's too early in my life. I'm too young to meet my soulmate. I need to go out with other boys first. If we meet now it might go all wrong because we're too young. You hear of that happening all the time.'

'What happened to "if it's meant to be you'll end up together"?'

'But in *Serendipity* they met at the wrong time first of all and didn't get together, but when they met again, years later, it was the right time and they lived happily ever after. If they'd got together at the beginning, by the end of the movie they'd probably be getting a divorce.'

'What are you talking about? That's a movie.'

'But movies are written by real people that these things have happened to.'

'So the guy who wrote *Night of the Living Dead* spent a lot of time with zombies when he was growing up?'

She gave me one of her looks. There was no arguing with her when she got in one of her moods. When Hannah made a decision it stayed made.

'Come on.' She headed in the opposite

direction, back to our table. I took one last look at the love of her life. He was checking out his reflection in the mirror behind the counter.

'I thought I told you to stay away from him.'

We heard Stacy's screeching voice before we saw her. We pushed our way through the crowd and got back to our table. Stacy was sitting opposite a scared-looking Sarah. Stacy's chavy mates stood next to her trying to look hard.

'I haven't been near him.' Sarah looked up and smiled with relief when she saw us.

'You were practically riding pillion on his quad bike this morning. Don't deny it, bitch. I have witnesses.'

'Have you been watching *The Bill* again, love?' I gave her mates filthy looks. They looked a little less confident.

'What?' Stacy snarled.

'"I have witnesses." How pathetic. You'll tell us to "shut it" next.'

She was about to say that exact thing and closed her mouth again really quickly and decided to launch in on Sarah again.

'Lucky for you your mates came back. You might not be so lucky next time.'

I'd heard enough. I grabbed her arm and yanked her so hard that she flew out of the chair and landed in a heap on the floor.

'I think you'll find you're sitting in my seat.'

She scrambled to her feet. Everyone was starting to look in our direction, including the staff. For a moment she stood her ground.

'How many times do I have to flush before you go away?' I took a step towards her.

The witty comeback was obviously not in her vocabulary. She gave Sarah the evils and headed for the door.

Hannah sat down next to Sarah.

'Are you OK?'

'Yeah, I'm fine. She's all talk, I hope.'

'You don't need to worry about her. She wouldn't dare touch you. And with your muscles you'd squash her head like a pea anyway.' I sat down and smiled at Sarah. I wished she'd stand up for herself a bit more.

'Where have you two been anyway? I thought you'd disappeared off the face of the planet.'

I sighed.

'Hannah was busy not meeting the love of her life.'

Sarah looked at me, then at the dreamy, goofy, 'brain missing in action' smile that was plastered all over Hannah's face, and then back to me.

'Tell me everything. Who? What? Where and how?'

'It's like a whole Hollywood movie packed into

five minutes, 'cept there's no happy ending,' I said.

'Yet.' Hannah leant forwards. She couldn't wait to let Sarah in on the great romance. I went and got the drinks. There was no danger of me falling in love on the way to the bar. Things like that didn't happen to people like me.

Sarah

We got back to our room with a second to spare before curfew. There was no way we could go to sleep, though. Hannah was too excited about Mr Mysterious as Nancy and me christened him.

We made up stories about who he could be and where they could meet again. He definitely wasn't staying at the château so that must mean he was a local, which also meant he would have a sexy French accent.

'Do you think he'd be a good kisser?' Hannah asked, as we all huddled together in our PJs.

'He's French. He's got to be a good kisser. They invented it.'

'You'll have to let us know, if you ever get near enough to find out.' Nancy shook her head. She couldn't understand why Hannah hadn't just gone up to the guy. But Nancy could do stuff like that. Hannah would rather wait forever rather than make the first move. I've always been like that, too, but sometimes waiting forever turns into never.

'Do you want him to be your first?' I asked.

Hannah blushed then nodded. 'Maybe.'

'Do you think Murphy could be yours?'

'No way.' I said it too sharply. Nancy gave me a look. Did she think I'd done it with Rhys already? She couldn't be further away from the truth.

'Who was your first, Nance?' Hannah asked.

She thought for a moment, then smiled.

'Mark Brunswick.'

'Where did you meet him?'

'He went to the boys' boarding school in the next village to my school. We all used to meet in the park after lessons.'

'He went to an all-boys boarding school?' Boarding school seemed like such a glamorous thing to me. Hollyoaks Comp. must seem like a right dump.

'Like I went to an all-girls boarding school and, no, it's nothing like Hogwart's before you ask.'

I shut my mouth again.

'Did you fancy him straight away?' Hannah was on a roll.

'I thought he was cute. Definitely not the love of my life, though.'

'So did he ask you out or the other way round?'

'We just sort of got together.'

'And how long were you together before you did it?'

'A few weeks. I can't exactly remember.'

Hannah looked at me and grinned. We talked about sex quite a bit. Not as much as boys do, I'm sure, but it did seem to sneak into our conversations more and more often. It was the big unknown to her and me. I mean, we read about it and saw it in films and heard other people talk about 'doing it' but neither of us had ever got close. I knew who I wanted my first to be, even though he was way more experienced. Now it seemed Hannah knew who she wanted it to be, too. It was suddenly more real than ever before. One day it would happen, and that was a pretty scary thought.

'So?' Hannah's voice dropped to a whisper. 'What was it actually like?'

Nancy stayed quiet for a moment.

'I don't remember that much about it really. Just that it was a bit awkward. Neither of us really knew what we were doing, where to stick what and when. And it was all over pretty quick. The earth didn't move, angels didn't sing in the heavens and bolts of lightening didn't fire down from the sky. Sorry. We were just glad to get it over with.'

We must both have looked so disappointed that she smiled.

'It was better the second time. When we weren't both so nervous. And it got much better as we got to know each other.'

'So the better you know someone?' I heard myself asking.

'I think so.' Nancy nodded. 'You definitely don't want to do it with just anyone.'

She looked pointedly at me.

'And you want to make sure they feel the same way about you.'

'I'm going to wait until I get married,' Hannah said.

We both gave her a look.

'OK, maybe I'll wait until I meet the guy I'm going to marry.'

'You might be waiting for years,' I pointed out, as practical as ever.

'Unless Mr Mysterious is your intended.' Nancy grinned.

'I didn't even see him. What was he like?' I'd been too busy being ranted at by Stacy.

'He's gorge, isn't he Nance?' Hannah looked all dreamy and romantic. Nancy winced at me, quickly so Hannah wouldn't see. It told me everything I needed to know. Mr Mysterious was no Greek God. But if Hannah liked him that was good enough. She couldn't understand what people saw in Rhys so it stood to reason that one person's Robbie Williams was another person's Robbie Fowler.

'He's got beautiful eyes and the cutest hair.' Hannah was reliving her big moment right in front of us. 'The crowd parted and I saw him and he saw me and our eyes just locked like we were the only people in the room. My heart was going crazy. I've never had a feeling like that in my entire life.'

'And yet you wouldn't go and talk to him.' Nancy rolled her eyes.

'I couldn't. And, anyway, he should have been the one to come up to me.'

'Hello! This is the twenty-first century. Girls are allowed to make the first move. In fact, it's almost compulsory. Boys are so useless that if you left it to them you'd never snog anyone.' There was no arguing with Nancy's logic. Boys were pretty useless.

'You might be able to go up and ask someone out but I can't.' Hannah was started to get annoyed.

'Why not?' As usual Nancy didn't notice when she was starting to irritate someone.

'Because they might say no,' Hannah answered, her voice short and clipped. I could tell she didn't want to talk about this any more.

'So what if they do? You've not lost anything.'

Hannah fixed Nancy with one of her looks. An argument was brewing.

'You do it all the time, I suppose.'

'If I see someone I fancy.'

'So how come, if you're so confident and not bothered about being knocked back, you haven't been out with a lad in the whole time we've known you?'

Nancy jumped up off the bed.

'Because the boys in Hollyoaks suck. If I saw someone I liked I would ask him out. But I don't just go out with anyone. And, anyway, I snogged Justin at New Year.'

'Doesn't count.'

'Yeah it does.'

'No it doesn't, because you never actually went out.'

'Still snogged him.'

'Which you only did because you knew Nicole still liked him and you wanted to prove you were better than her.'

'That's not why I did it.'

'Yeah it was.'

'No it wasn't.'

They were both on their feet now. I sat on the bed and watched them square up to each other.

I wished I were a million miles away. I hate it when people argue. Even when it's nothing to do with me it makes me want to bury my head under my duvet and cry.

I hear Mum and Dad arguing downstairs some nights at home. It's horrible. They've always argued, ever since I can remember. Well, Mum argues and Dad sits there and takes it mostly, but it's got worse lately. I sometimes wonder if they'll split up, but then, next day, everything seems fine again.

I asked Dad once if they would ever get divorced. He just laughed and said that they loved each other. Every marriage goes through ups and downs. It was quite normal and nothing to worry about. It's a depressing thought. Is that what we all have to look forward to when we get married? Why would you marry someone you spend so much time fighting with?

Amy, my little sister, says that if they did get divorced it might not be such a bad thing. They'd both feel so guilty we could get them to buy us anything we wanted. Plus, she said, one of her school friends gets two lots of birthday and Christmas presents and two lots of holidays. I don't care about any of that. I don't want my parents to split up, because then I'd have to choose which one to live with. Except this is my life we're talking about so I wouldn't get a choice. I'd have to live with Mum. Without Dad there to protect me it would be horrific. They couldn't ever split up. I forced the thought out of my head.

'You'd do anything to be centre of attention.' Hannah was on her feet now and their voices were loud enough to be heard in the corridor outside.

'Me? You're the one "Oh, I've met the man of my dreams but I can't talk to him."'

'How does that make me centre of attention?'

'Because you want us all to crowd round you and tell you how great you are and how he's bound to fancy you because you're so perfect.'

Hannah waved her hand at Nancy.

'Whatever. Mentalist.'

'I'm not the one who has my whole life planned out in the back of my diary.' Nancy suddenly stopped talking, knowing she'd gone too far.

'How do you know about that?' Hannah had gone very pale, her eyes very wide. 'Have you read my diary? I'll kill you if you have.'

'I haven't touched your stupid diary.' Nancy flushed red. 'Josh told me. Ages ago.'

Hannah looked like her head was about to explode. Then she flung herself on to her bed, turned her light off and pretended to go to sleep.

'He was just being an annoying little brother. I don't think he'd actually read it,' Nancy offered, trying to make the peace. Hannah didn't say anything. Conversation over.

Nancy looked at me and shrugged. I don't think she has any idea how she gets herself in these situations. She just opens her mouth and all this stuff comes out that she has no control over. World War Three erupts and Nancy is still clueless as to how she managed to start it.

'I'm going to get a drink.' She pulled on her dressing gown and slippers and headed out of the room.

'You OK, Han?' I asked when she'd gone.

'I'm sleeping,' came her muffled response.

'Nancy didn't mean anything.'

'I know.' Hannah turned over to look at me. 'Thing is, in a way she's right. I've never really had a proper boyfriend, not since Andrew Drake at primary school. Maybe I do need to live in the real world a bit more. It's not like Orlando Bloom is going to come knocking on my door, is it?'

She sighed and flopped back on to the pillow. I wanted to tell her that sometimes the real world is overrated. In the real world you get let down and disappointed by people. Sometimes dreaming about things was better than the reality.

Nancy

I'd done it again. Got into an argument without intending to. All I'd wanted to do was to make Hannah see that she should have gone up and talked to Mr Mysterious. That you had to grab opportunities when they came along just in case they never came along again.

I went into the common room at the end of the hall, got myself a can of Coke from the machine and sat at the big table. I picked out one of the magazines from the big pile. I'd sit there and read it until Hannah and Sarah had both fallen asleep.

The first magazine I opened had one of those stupid quizzes. It was called 'How good a friend are you?' Mostly As and you're the best friend anyone could have; mostly Bs, you're a good friend but sometimes a bit thoughtless; mostly Cs, you're a fair-weather friend, only there in the good times; and mostly Ds, who needs enemies when they've got friends like you.

I quickly put the magazine back on top of the pile. Then I took it from the top and shoved it in the middle so I couldn't see it. I didn't need a quiz to tell me what sort of friend I was. I was pretty sure I'd be a mostly Ds kind of girl.

'It's very late.' I hadn't notice the door swing open. Miss Rousseau stepped in and folded her arms. I was certain I was about to get flamed. It would round the day off perfectly.

Instead she sat down next to me.

'Are you feeling unwell?'

I looked at her. Had I heard right? Was she being nice? The stories we'd heard from some of others – who'd heard them from other people who'd stayed at the centre before – made her out to be the non-magical equivalent of Professor McGonagall. Not that I'd read the Harry Potter books. I had better things to do with my life than read about a geeky nerd who flies around on a broomstick. Give me a Golf GTi any day.

I like books about real people and stuff that could really happen. I'd never admit it to Becca but I loved *Lady Chatterley's Lover* and not just for the rude bits. My all-time favourite book though is *Wuthering Heights*. All that love and betrayal and tortured heroine stuff is fab. Much better than the pap Hannah likes to read where all the endings are happy ones.

'Nancy?'

I realized that I hadn't answered her question, too busy picturing myself running over wild and desolate moors to meet my Heathcliff, who looked strangely like Murphy.

'I'm fine, Miss. I was just thirsty.'

Miss Rousseau smiled. How could anyone

think she was a fearsome battleaxe type creature? In a funny way she reminded me of Becca. She had that inner peace quality that only certain people have. Like they've got life all figured out.

'My name is Adrianne. It's OK to call me that when I'm not working.'

'Thanks.'

'So what is it that you and your friends have been arguing about?'

'What makes you say that?'

'You were arguing when you arrived and now you're sitting here in the middle of the night on your own.' She did a little head tilt and shrug thing that was very French. I wondered if I could copy it. 'When girlfriends fall out it's normally because of boys.'

'I sometimes wish they didn't exist at all: boys, that is, not friends. I couldn't live without my friends. Even though I'm probably the crappest friend in the world.'

'I'm sure that's not true. If you weren't a good friend you wouldn't be sitting in here worrying about it.' She stood up. 'I am sure you are a very good friend and those are very hard to find. Have more faith in yourself.'

She smiled one last time, put a hand on my shoulder, just for a moment, and then headed for the door.

'Make sure you turn the light off before you go to bed.' Then she was gone. I heard her heels clipping down the hall. Maybe she was right. If I was a total lost cause in the friendship department I wouldn't give a single toss about what the others thought of me and I certainly wouldn't feel guilty about getting into an argument that I wasn't sure I started in the first place. I resolved that the next day I would not fall out with anyone, especially now I had two missions to accomplish. The first was to get Sarah with Murphy and the second to get Hannah with Mr Mysterious. Two such selfless acts were sure to gain me lots of good karma and then, who knows, my own Mr Mysterious might walk into my life.

We Still Can't Find What We're Looking For

TUESDAY

Hannah

I was drying my hair when Nancy woke up. I could see her reflection in the mirror.

'Sorry about last night,' she said.

'Me too.' I swivelled around to face her.

'I didn't mean any of it.'

'Yes you did.'

Her face fell. I smiled to let her know it was OK.

'But you were right. I should be more proactive with my life. Seeing Mr Mysterious was a sign.'

Nancy frowned.

'It was?'

'Yeah. A sign that I shouldn't just sit around and wait for things to happen.'

'Oh. Right. Good.'

I could tell I hadn't quite convinced her.

'So tonight we're going to go back to the café and I'm going to speak to him.'

'If he's there.'

'He will be. It's fate.'

'Fine. OK. Sounds like a good plan.'

'You've got to be there, though. When I ask him. Just in case.'

'Of course I'll be there. And Sarah. We're in this together, aren't we?' She smiled.

I grinned back.

'If she ever wakes up.'

We both looked at the lump under the duvet that was Sarah. I wondered what her Mum would say if she could see her. It was the first morning she'd missed her training. She was definitely making up for lost time on the whole sleep thing.

Nancy grabbed a pillow and chucked it at her. It bounced off and landed on the floor. Sarah grunted and wriggled and finally her eyes appeared over the top of the duvet.

'What time is it?' She sounded groggy.

'Time to get up. We've got to get the bus in an hour, so if you want breakfast . . .'

Sarah pulled the duvet back over her head.

Nancy grinned at me, leapt out of her bed and yanked Sarah's duvet on to the floor.

'Hey.' Sarah gave us both the daggers.

'Murphy will be there.' I winked at Nancy.

'Exactly.' Sarah groaned. 'And wherever he goes Schizo Stacy goes too.'

'She's no match for the three of us.' Nancy grabbed her towel and toothbrush.

'And we get a whole day in town. There's bound to be shops. I'm getting withdrawal symptoms. I feel the need to shop.' I looked at Sarah. 'Don't you want to shop? Clothes, shoes, bags? All that French chic, ours for the taking . . . well, buying anyway.'

We were spending the day in the town of Reims. It was about an hour's drive on the bus. Full of historical buildings and museums, Mr Lang had told us. It was the place where the Germans had surrendered to Eisenhower and ended the Second World War. More importantly, it was much bigger than the pokey little village down the road. Pokey little villages were fine when meeting Mr Mysterious across a crowded room. In fact, pokey little villages were best for that because it would be much easier for fate to engineer it for us to bump into each other again. But for shopping bigger was definitely better. I'd purposely left room in my suitcase for two pairs of shoes, a couple of new tops and a jacket if I could afford one. And there was Rhys complaining my suitcase was too heavy on the way out here. Wait until he came and picked me up. Then he'd know what a heavy suitcase really felt like.

'I suppose. I'm still so tired, though. I think I could sleep for twenty-four hours a day.'

'It's all those years of early mornings at the pool.' Nancy paused at the door, 'If you add them up, you're probably a few months of sleep behind everyone else.'

She skipped out of the door. I was glad she was in a bubbly mood. I had a great feeling about the day. I'd buy a new top to wow Mr Mysterious with, maybe some perfume, too, and when we went to the café that evening I would go straight up to him, no messing, and ask him out. He'd say yes and our romance would be born. The thought of it made me smile like an idiot.

'What?' Sarah clawed her way out of bed.

'Just thinking.'

'About your mystery man?'

'Who else? Hey, imagine if I get with him and you get with Murphy. Wouldn't that be cool?'

'Yeah.' But she didn't sound convinced. I knew what it was. She was worried about Nancy.

'We won't leave Nance out, though. Maybe

we could find her someone. Have you seen anyone that might be suitable?'

'Not really.'

'We'll check everyone out again when we're on the coach. We might have missed someone from the other school. What are Murphy's mates like?'

'You mean Ant and Dec?'

'They might not be that bad, if we get a closer look. They might be the sort that grow on you. Like Dominic Monaghan.'

'Who?'

'The guy who's in *Lord of the Rings* and *Lost*. You wouldn't have looked twice at him when he was a hobbit, but as a ship-wrecked rock star he's quite cute. He grows on you, don't you think?'

Sarah looked at me as if I were crazy.

'Yeah. Not really seeing that.'

We had to break off to get ready, otherwise we really would have missed the bus. But once we were safely sitting on the back seats and the bus was speeding through the French countryside we really got into the whole 'weird people you fancy' topic.

'Martin Freeman from *The Office*,' Nancy said after a moment's thought. 'It's that whole crumpled look he has. And he's funny.'

'Ewww.' I pulled a face.

'Your turn then.' Nancy grinned at me.

'Richard Hammond.'

'Who?' Nancy looked puzzled.

'The little guy off *Top Gear*. It's Rhys's favourite TV show,' I corrected her.

'He is quite cute,' Sarah added. 'Not that I really watch *Top Gear* or anything.'

'You've got to choose one of your own.' I wasn't going to share Richard with anyone.

'Gary Lineker,' she said, after a moment's thought.

'Seriously?' Nancy and me were trying to stop ourselves from laughing out loud.

'I've had a crush on him since I was five.' She went red as she said it.

That did it. We all burst out laughing. Everyone on the bus, including Mr Lang and Miss O'Donnell, turned around to see what was going on.

'Leave him alone. He's lovely. And he's a nice person. And he was a great footballer,' Sarah said through her giggles.

'I've got another secret crush,' I found myself saying. 'My first love, Jonathan Ross. I like his hair.'

That brought more howls of laughter. We were all doubled up.

'Stop it, I'm going to wee myself,' Nancy said breathlessly.

It was so great when it was like this. At that moment I was totally and utterly happy. I had the best friends in the world.

Nancy

As we drove into Reims our spirits sank to our shoes. The way Hannah had gone on about shops and French style we were all expecting a mini-Paris. Instead, we drove past steam-bellowing factories and depressing concrete apartment blocks. Not exactly the Champs Élysées. It didn't help that the sky was a horrible dirty grey colour. It was the sort of day made for hot baths, big bars of chocolates and marathon DVD-watching sessions.

Mr Lang and Miss O'Donnell trooped us off the coach and got us to stand around at the entrance to a big park. There was an outdoor ice rink, which almost looked tempting, but otherwise we were all about as enthusiastic as a bunch of lab rats. About half the people from Hollyoaks Comp. had come on the trip. The rest had opted for a day out at some Second World War cemetery. Barrel of laughs, that one. The rest of the group was made up of people from the other school, including Stacy and her pathetic chav mates and Murphy with his Ant and Dec buddies.

The only silver lining of the whole thing was Murphy. He kept looking over, sometimes at Sarah, but once or twice I caught him looking at me. He even smiled and mouthed the word 'boring' as Mr Lang gave us this speech about the importance of Reims in the history of France. Yawn. Even Mr Lang seemed half-hearted. I'm pretty sure all he wanted to do was tell us all to bog off so he could head to the nearest bar.

'OK. Now you've had the history lesson, here's the objective of today's outing.'

Hannah, Sarah and me all looked at each other in alarm. Objective? We all thought we were here to eat, drink and shop.

'It's a scavenger hunt. You'll split up into teams of four. Each team will be given a letter of the alphabet. The objective is for you to collect – legally – as many articles beginning with that letter as you can, in either French or English. There'll be a prize for the team who collects the most things and a prize for the team with the most unusual or ingenious thing. We'll meet back here at 3pm. Any questions?'

'What's the prize, sir?' Sarah asked, making Hannah and me look at her. What did it matter what the prize was; we were going shopping not wasting time on a scavenger hunt.

'You'll find out at 3pm. Can you split your-selves off into groups, please?'

I looked at Sarah.

'You're not serious about this?'

'Why not?'

'Because I want to go shopping,' Hannah replied.

'We can shop at the same time. Come on. It'll be fun. You don't want Schizo girl to beat us, do you?'

We all looked round at Stacy, who was in deep conversation with her chavettes.

'Good point,' I said, then I had one of my brilliant ideas. 'But we're one member short. Who can we possibly ask?'

Hannah suddenly went pale.

'Please not him.'

Beaky was heading over to us, his head floating above the crowd. I wondered if oxygen was in short supply up there and that was why stringing a sentence together was such hard work. We definitely didn't want to be stuck with him all day.

'I've got a much better idea.' I got hold of both of them and dragged them to where Murphy was standing. I tapped him on his shoulder.

'Fancy joining our team?' He turned, frowned for a moment, then looked at Ant and Dec. They were playing football with a crumpled up Coke can. Ant tried to kick it, got his legs tangled together and cannoned into Dec, so they both went flying.

Murphy turned back to us with a big grin.

'Try and stop me.'

I gave Sarah and Hannah a look. Result or what? Hannah looked impressed, as she should, but Sarah just gave me the daggers.

'What are you doing?' she whispered in one of those loud whispers people do when they're really annoyed at you.

'Trust me,' I said. I didn't want Murphy to hear. It was still my plan to get them together, even though it was pretty clear Sarah wasn't interested. But when I set out to do something I get it done. And Sarah might not relish the thought of spending the day with Murphy, but I did. He was looking extra cute, wearing a beanie hat and a cool Lacoste jacket. Not that I'm into designer labels. I mean, why pay a fortune for something just to act as a free advertising space for the designer? They should pay us to wear their stuff. But even I couldn't deny that designer gear looked great on Murphy. A black bin bag would look great on Murphy.

'Who's in your team?' Mr Lang came up to us with his clipboard. He wrote down our names. 'Team name?'

'Charlie's Angels?' Hannah piped up. She really did have a thing for pap movies.

Murphy screwed up his face pretending to be offended.

'Hey, that's sexist. I'm a member of this team, too. How about Murphy's Angels?'

He winked at me. My heart did this weird double-thud thing. What was that about?

'There's no such thing as Murphy's Angels,' Sarah pointed out. She was in a huff. I could tell.

'There is now,' Mr Lang said as he scribbled the name down. 'Your team can have the letter C.'

He moved on to the next group, which happened to be Stacy and the chavettes. She'd already clocked that Murphy had hooked up with us and you could almost see the steam shooting out of her ears. I waved at her as she glared over. The day was picking up already.

'Things beginning with C, eh?' Murphy looked thoughtful, 'I can start us off. I have a little something in my wallet that fits perfectly.'

He said it staring straight at me with the most suggestive look on his face that I went bright red. Then he opened his wallet and waved a video membership card at us.

'Card begins with C, doesn't it? What did you think I meant?' He grinned at me, then gave Sarah a long lingering look. I noticed. She didn't. She was too busy checking her mobile phone for messages. I wondered for a moment if Rhys was keeping in contact.

'OK, you all know whose team you're in and

what letter you've got,' Mr Lang shouted above the din. 'So off you go. Try not to get arrested. See you back here at 3pm.'

Miss O'Donnell and him shared a look and watched as we all started to filter away. It suddenly hit me. Were they going off to have a shag somewhere? Urghh . . . I hoped not. Becca refused to tell me anything about them, even though the whole school knew they had a thing going. Whenever I brought it up Becca would just give me that look she gives me, the 'don't even go there' look, and say it was no one's business but their own. Of course, I took that as a big yes. Anyway, the simple fact is that teachers shouldn't be doing it with each other, or anyone else for that matter. And I'm including my sister in that. It's just wrong, and I didn't even want to think about it.

'Come on.' I linked arms with Hannah. 'Let's get a coffee first.'

'What about the scavenger hunt?' Sarah sidled away from Murphy, probably worried he'd try to link arms with her or something.

'Duh.' I rolled my eyes. 'Our letter is C. What letter does coffee begin with?'

'Oh, yeah.' Sarah looked sheepish.

We all headed towards the shopping area. I was sure that after spending a whole day together Sarah would look at Murphy in a new light. And when she did and they got together she'd better be grateful.

Sarah

How long did it take to drink coffee? It felt like we'd been in the café for hours. OK, maybe not hours, but I'd finished my drink ages ago. Hannah looked as fed up as I felt.

Nancy, on the other hand, was having a great time with Murphy. He was pretending to be French and speaking English in a very bad accent. It was kind of childish. People were looking round and shaking their heads. Nancy couldn't stop laughing.

'Shouldn't we get going?' I asked Hannah.

'Yeah. I need to go back to that shoe shop we passed and try on those shoes I saw.'

'I meant we should get going with the scavenger hunt.'

'Don't worry. We have our next item.' Murphy drained his cardboard coffee cup and held it up for us all to see.

'Having two things won't win us the competition.' I was itching to get up and race out of the shop. I can't help it. If there's a competition I always want to try and win. Even if we play Monopoly at home I still want to win. Mum's the same. Amy and Dad don't take games seriously, so it's always down to Mum and me. Then it's a 'take no prisoners' situation. We battle it out to the bitter end. I guess that means I take after my Mum, which isn't a nice thought because I don't want to be anything like her. Maybe I should try and be less competitive, but it's a bit like breathing or having brown hair. It's the way I was born and I can't help it.

'You're right.' Murphy smiled at me and held my gaze for longer than was necessary. I had to drag my eyes away. I felt myself blushing and nearly knocked my coffee off the table as I moved my hands out of reach of his. Just in case.

'You want to go to that shoe shop, Hannah?' He turned his attention to her, 'Are you going to buy some shoes?'

'I might.' She eyed him suspiciously. 'Why?'

'Because the French for shoes is *chaussures*. If you buy some that gives us three things without even trying.' He grinned triumphantly. You had to hand it to him. He had an answer for everything. I felt guilty again. I shouldn't even be thinking about Murphy.

We waited for Hannah as she tried on five different pairs of shoes. I got bored. I didn't have money to buy shoes and I wasn't in the mood to window shop. I went outside and checked my phone again. Nothing. I'd texted Rhys when we'd arrived at the château, just to let him know we were all safe. I thought he might have sent something back. I'd decided it was because of being in France and it had affected my phone, but then I'd got one of Amy's stupid jokes so I knew texts from back home were getting through. It had been nearly two days and normally when I text Rhys he texts straight back. Then a horrible thought hit me. Perhaps Hannah had been in touch with him. She could have told him about Murphy and me, even though there is no Murphy and me. In Rhys's eyes, Murphy could already be my boyfriend. My heart lurched. I felt sick. I had to text him.

Hi. Hope ur ok. Misin u. C u soon.
xx.

I hit send before I could change my mind and add more kisses or delete the two that I already had. In the moment after I sent it I felt relieved. Then, of course, you start to suffer from text lag. You time how long before it reaches the other person's phone, how long it would take for them to open it and read it. Then how long it would take for them to write a reply, hit send and then . . .

Nothing. That's when text lag sets in. That's when you start feeling awful again because you've taken the leap, sent the text and the ball's in their court. If they don't reply you feel rejected. Or you start to make up excuses. They didn't get your text, or they did send a reply but it never arrived. Or their phone is switched off. Or the battery is flat. Or they just hate you.

'What you doing?' Murphy stepped out of the shop. I realized I was still staring at my phone. I shoved it in my pocket, but kept one hand on it just in case.

'Nothing.'

'You're very different to other girls I know.' He looked back inside the shop. Nancy and Hannah were looking at two pairs of shoes, presumably trying to decide which ones to buy. 'Your life isn't ruled by shopping.'

'I do like shopping.' I felt uneasy. He was standing so close I could feel his breath on my cheek.

'But it doesn't rule your life. And that's a good thing,' He paused. I wanted to step away from him, but something held me there. I even looked up at him. His brown eyes were very serious. There was a lot of stuff going on in his head. You look at some people and there's nothing behind the eyes. Beaky's like that. 'Surface people', Nancy calls them. They do exactly what they say on the tin. The interesting people are the ones where the outside gives nothing away. I like Nancy's philosophies. Rhys has a lot going on under the surface. It'd just be nice if he'd share a bit more of it with me.

'Nancy says you're a champion swimmer. Do you swim for the county?'

'Yeah, and nationally.'

'God, you must be good. I used to swim a bit. I was OK but not good enough to ever get anywhere. I really admire anyone with a talent like that.'

'It's nothing special really. There's loads of people better than me.'

'Not that many if you swim at national level. I'm impressed. You must do a lot of training.'

'Loads. Sometimes it feels like it's all I ever do. I was supposed to keep my training up this week, but I haven't. My Mum will go ballistic when I get home.'

'Mums would be bored if we didn't do things to make them go crazy every so often. It's in their job description.'

I found myself laughing. My mobile started to vibrate and I came to my senses. I turned away from Murphy and dragged my phone out. It was a text but not from Rhys. It was from Dad.

Hope you are having fun. You don't
have to text me back. I just wanted
you to know everything was OK here.
Your Mum hasn't killed Amy or me
yet. Love, Dad

Parents really haven't got the hang of texting. All
his texts have correct spelling, grammar and
punctuation. Despite my disappointment it made
me smile.

'Boyfriend?' Murphy asked.

'My Dad,' I said without thinking.

He smiled. I should have lied, said yes.

'I'm going to hurry those two up.' I made my
excuses and leapt back into the shop. I felt
strange. How come I'd started to open up to this
guy who I barely knew? And why did I feel so
comfortable around him? It wasn't right.

Hannah

I was getting really fed up. The day wasn't going
as planned at all. Nancy was practically ignoring
me; too busy messing around with Murphy, who
kept doing silly walks and stupid accents.

And Sarah was just being dead stroppy.

I thought we'd all agreed that we were going
to spend the day shopping, but every time I

wanted to go into a shop she pulled a face. I know that makes me sound horrible, but scavenger hunts were so childish and pointless. I had to find something nice to wear that evening, but no one else seemed interested. Sarah was fixated on winning, walking everywhere at three million miles an hour, collecting cards, a free sample of cheese from a deli, a cap off a bottle of Coke.

She even picked up an empty cigarette packet (ewww . . .) and spent ten minutes trying to persuade a guy to donate his cap. Eventually he gave in and Sarah waved the cap around like she'd won an Olympic medal.

'We might even stand a chance of winning now,' she said.

'Be worth it to see Schizo Stacy's face.' Nancy held open the carrier bag we'd been putting all our things in. Apart from my shoes. They weren't going in the same bag as a grotty old fag packet and an empty coffee cup.

'Technically speaking, as we're in France,' I said, 'it's not a cap. It's a beret and therefore it doesn't begin with C.'

It was a petty thing to say, but after two hours of trailing round in the cold, passing loads of great shops full of beautiful people and amazing clothes, I'd had enough.

Murphy, Nancy and Sarah all stared at me like

I'd told them they all smelt of dead dog or putrid cat.

'If you think you could do so much better you try being in charge.' Sarah pulled a face.

'No thanks. And who put you in charge anyway?' I snapped back.

'No one else wanted to do it. Every team needs a leader.'

'We came here to go shopping, not take part in a stupid childish game.'

'It's not stupid or childish. Even big companies use scavenger hunts as team-building exercises. My Dad used to do them.'

'I bet he only did them because he had to. Nobody would volunteer for this. Except you.'

'I think it's fun. We're having a laugh anyway,' Nancy chipped in. Murphy nodded in agreement. He looked uncomfortable, though. In my experience no lad likes to be in the vicinity of girls bitching at each other. Rhys says it's because guys always end up getting dragged into the argument and whatever the guy says it's always wrong. The guy then ends up getting the blame for the entire thing.

'You might be having fun but I'm not. I'm cold and bored and fed up. All I want to do is go shopping.'

'You've been miserable all morning.' Nancy looked at me coldly. 'If you haven't got anything constructive to say try not saying anything at all.'

'Fine,' I replied.

'Good.' Nancy jutted her chin out. It was stalemate.

'Right. I'm going shopping then. Who's coming?' I didn't even bother looking at Sarah, but I thought Nancy would choose to come with me, especially as it would leave Sarah alone with Murphy.

Tumbleweed rolled past. No one said a word. But I couldn't back down now. I had no choice, even though the last thing on the planet I wanted to do was go off on my own in a strange town where everyone spoke a different language to me.

'I'll go on my own then.' Maybe a threat would work.

Still nothing. I'd dug myself so deep that I was practically in Australia.

'I'm going, then.'

I could tell by Sarah and Nancy's faces that they didn't believe I would actually go through with it. They thought I'd chicken out.

'See you then.' I paused one long last time, hoping one of them would say something. They didn't. I took a deep breath, drew myself up as tall as I could, spun on my heel and walked away down the street as chicly and elegantly as I knew how. As I went my heel caught in one of the cobbles and I pitched forward, then sideways as my feet tried to catch up with my body. I scrabbled to regain my balance, arms waving everywhere like a demented duck, and managed to avoid falling on my bum. I righted myself and carried on walking as if nothing had happened, but my cheeks flamed red and I knew Nancy and Sarah, and probably Murphy, too, would be killing themselves laughing.

I stormed down the street, turned one corner then another and another. Only then did I feel safe enough to stop. Even better I was right outside a boutique. Who needed friends anyway? I went into the boutique, and the bag shop next door and the perfumery on the opposite side of the street, then a bit further down was this incredible patisserie with the most incredible cakes and pastries. No Cornish pasties, egg custards, cornflake cakes or iced fingers here. If style started with what you ate it was little wonder the French were leagues ahead of the British.

I stepped out of the patisserie with a selection of pastries. The girls would love me for bringing back such delicacies. All argument forgotten, I decided to head back and rejoin them. I'd done enough shopping to keep me happy for now. Of course I looked up and down the street and realized not only did I have no idea where I was, or even what direction I'd come from, but I had absolutely no clue how to get back to the 3pm meeting place. I was utterly and completely lost.

My heart started to flutter in my chest. People hurried past me. Car horns blared. My lungs started to tighten. I felt like I was going to have a panic attack. I know that sounds pathetic, but I have good reason. When I was five I got lost in the Arndale Centre in Manchester. Mum had been trying some shoes on Josh and I'd got bored and wandered off. Ever since then I've had a fear of getting lost.

My hands were trembling as I got my mobile out of my bag to call Sarah and Nancy. But how pathetic would I sound? 'Please come and find me.' 'Where are you?' 'I don't know, I'm lost.'

Nancy would never let me forget it. She was so independent if she got lost she'd think it was a laugh. In fact she'd probably not even realize she was lost as she'd be so busy enjoying herself. She certainly wouldn't let it worry her. I wasn't a baby any more. I was sixteen, far too old to be getting lost and then crying about it. I would sort this mess out myself.

I took some deep breaths, glanced at my lovely new shoes, all wrapped in tissue paper in their box, and started to walk. This was all part of the new me, surviving on my own, doing things for myself. If I walked around the streets for long enough I'd be bound to see something or someone I recognized. Eventually. Of course if I didn't get back to the meeting place by 3pm the coach would leave without me and I'd be stuck here. I'd spent all my money on the shoes so I'd have to sleep on the streets. I'd probably get mugged, or worse, and I would never get to see Mr Mysterious again, let alone talk to him. I felt my lungs tightening again. I clutched my bags close to my side and quickened my step. I could do this.

Sarah

After Hannah stormed off we all stood and looked at each other for a moment. I think we all expected her to turn round and come back but she didn't.

'She'll have to catch us up later,' Nancy said. 'Come on.'

We went into the huge Notre Dame cathedral (we'd all thought it was in Paris but apparently they were all over the place in France; a bit like Starbucks – one on every corner) where Nancy put some money in the donation box and got a candle. I was convinced she was going to nick a prayer cushion. She started to shove it down her top, but she was only messing. It made Murphy laugh so loud that everyone looked in our direction. One of the priests started walking towards us, so we legged it.

Our next stop was a bar. Through the window we'd seen a big round red-faced guy with a huge beard smoking a cigar. We watched for a few minutes. He'd take a huge drag on the thing, then hold it away from his mouth and blow out perfect smoke rings that looked just like giant polo mints.

We all looked at each other.

'Cigar,' Nancy said.

'Cigar.' Murphy nodded in reply.

'Leave it to me.' Nancy grinned and slipped inside the bar. We watched her walk past the man and then sit at the neighbouring table. She was going to wait this one out and then retrieve the stub. Urghhh . . .

'She's a bit crazy, isn't she?' Murphy said in my ear. He was standing close again.

'A little. You never know what she's going to do next.' I glanced up at him.

'Unpredictable.'

'Just a bit.'

'What about you? Are you up for taking chances?'

'Depends what it is.' I kept my eyes firmly on Nancy. She looked over and smiled. It occurred to me that she'd left us alone on purpose.

'Nancy says you definitely don't have a boyfriend.'

I said nothing, but I resolved to kill Nancy the first opportunity I got.

'I didn't believe her. How could someone as beautiful as you be single?'

I looked at him.

'Do you practise being cheesy or does it come naturally?'

He went red and smiled.

'That was bad wasn't it? Sorry.' He touched my arm, 'I meant it, though. You are beautiful and it's a crime that you're single.'

'I'm not. Single that is.'

'But Nancy said . . .'

'Nancy doesn't know everything about me.'

He studied me for a moment.

'Secret boyfriend, eh? Is that who you were texting before?'

'That's none of your business.'

Inside, Nancy was now talking to the waiter and gesturing towards cigar man.

'Sorry. Again. Seems like I'm always putting my foot in it with you.'

'Forget about it.'

'Can I ask you one last thing, though? You can

say yes or no, though obviously I'd prefer you to say yes, but if you do say no I'll never bug you again, OK?'

I didn't reply. My heart was pounding and I was willing Nancy to rip the damn cigar out of the man's mouth and run outside with it.

'I'll take your silence as a yes. OK. Big moment here. Would you, could you, possibly consider going out with me tonight? There's a French film on at the cinema in the village, *Jules et Jim*. It's about two men who fall in love with the same beautiful woman. It's great.'

I stared at him. Had he really just asked me out? My stomach lurched. Nancy was still talking to the waiter.

'OK. Not quite the response I was looking for. Could I take your silence as a yes again?'

'No,' I almost shouted back. 'Absolutely one-hundred per cent no.'

The smile disappeared off his face.

'Say it like you mean it.' He was hurt. 'Don't pull any punches. I'm not that repulsive, am I? I got the impression you liked me.'

'Where from? I'm not interested in you.'

'Come on. You've been flirting with me all day.'

'No I haven't. I've barely even talked to you. You've been too busy messing around with Nancy.'

'Jealous?'

'What? You must be joking.'

'Why are you getting so angry then?' The smug look on his face made me want to slap him. I was so angry I couldn't even get any words out. I pushed past him and started walking up the street. Nancy came running out of the bar as I went past. She was clutching the cigar stub like a sixty-a-day smoker.

'What's going on?' she asked me. I didn't slow my pace.

'Ask him.' I didn't bother to look back. I wanted to put as much space between Murphy and me as possible.

Nancy

I watched Sarah stomp away down the street. Then I looked at Murphy. What on earth had he done to her?

'Don't look at me,' he said. 'I did nothing.'

'Doesn't look like it.' I looked back up the street, but Sarah had already disappeared.

'I started asking her about boyfriends and she went all weird. I thought you said she was single.'

'She is single. Sort of. Mostly. It's a very long story.'

'She's seeing someone she shouldn't be?'

'I'd rather not talk about it.'

'Fair enough. Why do girls have to make everything so complicated?'

'We don't. Things only get complicated when boys get involved. If you ceased to exist us girls would never fall out with each other.'

He narrowed his eyes thoughtfully.

'I find that very hard to believe.'

'It's true.'

'I thought Hannah went off in a sulk because she wanted to shop. Shopping's nothing to do with boys.'

'You're so wrong. She only wanted to shop so badly because she needs nice things to wear to impress guys. Your fault again.'

'Basically, whatever I say, you'll be able to twist it around to make it the fault of the entire male race.'

'Yep.'

He started laughing.

'I like you. You're funny.'

'Funny girls are normally so underrated.'

'Not by me. Plus you're standing in the middle of a street holding the butt end of a sweaty man's cigar. That's pure class in my book.'

I looked at the cigar butt. I'd almost forgotten I was holding it. It was truly disgusting.

'Open the bag,' I directed Murphy. He held

the bag open and I deposited the butt in with the rest of our collection.

'What now? We've still got a couple of hours to kill.' He looked at me, deep into my eyes, 'It's pretty rank out here and I'm freezing. Got anything in mind to pass the time?'

He might as well have asked me if I wanted to go to bed with him. Or maybe I was reading too much into it. My heart skipped a beat anyway.

'We could, erm . . . find a café?'

'Perfect.' He grinned, and we walked down the street, shoulders almost touching. I wanted to grab his hand, but didn't quite have the nerve.

'This'll do very nicely.' He flopped down on to a big leather sofa in the corner of a large, gloomy coffee shop. I flopped next to him. We were in a booth, hidden from sight from most of the rest of the shop.

'How's your latte?' he asked as I took a sip.

'Fab.'

At that moment I saw a movement out of the corner of my eye. I glanced round to see Mr Lang and Miss O'Donnell sit down in another booth. From where I was sitting I could just see them, via their reflection in a large mirror.

'Oh, my God.' I shuffled closer to Murphy, just in case they could see me.

'What?' He didn't seem to mind my sitting a bit closer.

'Two of my teachers. Having coffee.'

'They are allowed to drink. And this is a coffee shop.'

'No, but look at them.'

He leant across me and put a hand on my leg for balance. I could smell a vague hint of musky aftershave. I hadn't been so close to a lad since my New Year's pash with Justin. It gives you that tingly feeling like you don't know what's going to happen but you can't wait to find out.

'Where? Oh God. I can see them. What *are* they doing? Oh . . . that is disgusting.'

Mr Lang smoothed the hair from Miss O'Donnell's face and then leant across to kiss her. We both watched as she closed her eyes, enjoying the moment. Then Mr Lang broke away to smile at her. She giggled and started to turn her head in my direction. Murphy and me sprung back into our booth and huddled together, hoping we hadn't been seen.

'They're teachers, for God's sake. They shouldn't be having sex at all. Not even with each other. There's laws against that in some American States.' Murphy pulled a face and pulled me closer to him. Somehow he'd managed to put his arm round me without me noticing. Normally I would have pulled away – it's not like I invited him to touch me and I hate people invading my personal space without asking first – but for some reason it felt really comfortable.

'I reckon he's been having his own themed scavenger hunt while we've been wandering the streets,' Murphy said, still not moving his arm away, 'But it wasn't letters of the alphabet he was looking for.'

'Looks like he found whatever he was looking for.' I giggled. 'And by the way she's smiling I think he won first prize.'

'Urghh. Please stop. I'm getting all sorts of unpleasant images in my mind. I'll never be able to look at a teacher in the same way again.'

'I don't now. My sister's a teacher. At my school.'

'Really? That must be well weird. Does she take you for anything?'

'English lit. She's OK, though . . . for a teacher.'

'Bet you can get away with all sorts of things.'

'Not really. She's stricter on me than the others.'

'Yeah? That sucks. What happened to family loyalty?'

'I have no idea.'

'So what's your sister like? And if she's as pretty as you why is Mr Lang shagging that old dog rather than her?' He grinned.

'She's married. Otherwise, I'm sure he would

much prefer her to Hagrid,' I said, then I realized that he'd just said I was pretty and I felt myself smiling like an idiot.

'Married, huh? Well at least one sister is still available. Unless you've got a secret boyfriend, too?'

'Nope. No boyfriend, secret or otherwise.' I looked into his eyes. For a moment I thought he was going to lean forward and kiss me, but he just smiled.

'Your coffee's getting cold.' He withdrew his arm and picked up his own coffee. I couldn't keep the disappointment off my face. For a moment I'd thought something good might happen to me for a change. But no. Wrong again. He was probably pining after Sarah, who wasn't even interested in him, despite all my hard work. Life was so unfair. I gazed into my coffee wishing I could jump in and disappear.

'So, erm . . . I was wondering . . . there's a French film on at the cinema in the village tonight, *Jules et Jim*. It's about two men who fall in love with the same beautiful woman. It's great. I'd really love it if you'd come with me. I'll even buy the popcorn. If they have popcorn in France.'

I nearly dropped my coffee mug. I looked across at him, convinced the words I'd heard were a figment of my imagination.

'What?' I could barely speak.

'Cinema. Tonight. You and me. What d'you say?'

I wanted to leap around the room and scream out loud. He'd just asked me out. This totally fit boy who could have any girl he wanted had just asked me out. But I forced myself to remain calm. I was a cool chick. Nothing fazed me. That's probably why he liked me.

'Sure. Why not?' I said as casually as I could manage. I picked up my coffee, trying not to shake, and took a sip.

'Great. We can meet outside the cinema. About seven o'clock?'

'Cool.'

And that was that. I had myself a date. We waited for Mr Lang and Miss O'Donnell to leave, and then we went too. He held my hand as we walked outside, which felt weird but great. We both let go as we got back on to the street. I hadn't forgotten that the original plan had been to get Murphy together with Sarah. I didn't want her to see us together; even if she wasn't interested in him it still felt a bit like I was doing the dirty on her. And it would be just as hard to explain it to Hannah. I was fed up of mis-understandings and I didn't want to fall out with them all again. No. It was much better to keep it quiet. Besides I didn't want to tempt fate. He could change his mind. I could get run over by a bus. If the date went well, maybe I would tell them then. For now, it would be my secret. If Sarah could keep secrets, so could I.

Sarah

It felt pretty good to storm off. I decided I should do it more often. Next time Mum was nagging at me because my swim times weren't good enough I'd give her the 'whatever' hand, spin on my heel and leave her with her mouth hanging open.

The satisfied feeling only lasted for a couple of minutes up until the moment I stopped and wondered what exactly I should do next. Storming off only really works if you have somewhere to storm off to, like your bedroom. You need a door to slam, a bed to throw yourself down on and a stereo to play some music at three thousand decibels.

Instead, I found myself standing in the middle of an unfamiliar street, in a foreign city with a couple of hours before the coach was due to take us back to the château. What on earth was I going to do for the next two hours, one hundred and twenty minutes or seven thousand two hundred seconds? I thought about ringing Hannah, but then figured she was probably still in a mood with me and wouldn't answer her phone. That reminded me that Rhys still hadn't texted back. I sighed. A woman with beautifully styled hair and incredibly high heels glided past me. She looked like one of those glamorous old Hollywood film stars that you see interviewed sometimes just after some even older star has died. She must have heard me sigh because she smiled sympathetically as she walked past. I got the feeling she knew I was sighing over a boy. I wondered how many boys she'd sighed over in her lifetime.

Why did we waste so much time being miserable because of the opposite sex? Life was passing me by while I waited for Rhys to make his mind up. He couldn't even take time out of his schedule to text me. He was probably out having fun and not even thinking about me. Although by now he could have sent me an email. He'd promised he would and I hadn't checked since yesterday morning. I might have been worrying over nothing. That was the moment I looked up and found I was standing right outside an Internet café. Fate was trying to tell me something. I smiled. It had to mean something.

I went inside, paid my money and set myself up at one of the screens. I had a really good positive feeling inside me. There had to be an email from him. The way he was when we last saw each other, the way he'd said he'd miss me, there was no way he wouldn't have emailed.

I entered my username and password (yeah, I admit, my password is IluvRhys, sad I know) and waited for the page to load. This time I didn't shut my eyes. I was confident.

I felt like I'd been hit in the face by a brick. There were three junk mails offering me money, a boob job and laser eye treatment, an update from the Robbie Williams website, but absolutely nothing from Rhys. My heart started to race with panic. In the league table of sayings 'absence makes the heart grow fonder' was seriously out-ranked by 'out of sight, out of mind'. It was like Chelsea v. Everton. Or even Chelsea v. Morecambe.

It was then I noticed the Instant Messenger Service. We used it loads. He was AnimalUnited and I was HustlerBabe. If he was online I'd know about it and he wouldn't be able to avoid me. That was the beauty of IMing.

I logged on and instantly my list of buddies came up. There was only one name on it. AnimalUnited.

He was there. My heart bounced about in my chest. All my fingers felt like fat sausages as I tried to type. Somehow I managed to write:

Bonjour. How ru?

I hit send and waited . . .

And waited . . .

And waited until I thought I was going to throw up. Then a reply flashed up.

Hey u. Havin fun?

I grinned. I could picture him sitting in front of a computer screen at college. I wondered what he'd be wearing. Probably his leather jacket that looked so sexy and some ripped jeans.

It's ok. Be more fun if u were here.

I hit send and sat there like a geek with the biggest smile on my face.

Again, it seemed like forever for the reply to spring on to the screen.

Soz. Gotta go. Lecture. Take it easy. C ya 18r.

I blinked at it for a few moments. I was certain he'd pressed send too soon. There must be more to come than that. I even forgot to breathe. And then there was the sound of a door slamming and a service message flashed up 'AnimalUnited has logged out.' My online buddies list was empty.

I couldn't move. Every part of my body was frozen. Take it easy? C ya l8r? No 'I wish I was there with you' or 'I'm missing you' or even one single lousy 'x'. It was like he was IMing someone he'd never met, some person he was trading some music with over the net. I obviously didn't mean anything to him at all. He'd given me nothing. Even if he'd been with Gilly he could have put one kiss or done something to show he was missing me.

I logged out and got to my feet. My legs felt weak. I felt sick to the stomach. Everything I'd dreamt about Rhys and me, everything I'd imagined, was all shattered. He wasn't missing me. He didn't even want to know me.

'Are you OK?'

I spun round.

Hannah was standing just behind me, smiling. 'You look really pale.'

'No . . . I'm . . . I'm fine . . .' I forced myself to look as normal as possible. I took all my disappointment and misery, folded it all up and shoved it right to the back of my mind, into the room where I hide things like that. I struggled but I managed to shut the door.

'Where's Nancy?' Hannah asked. She glanced down at my computer screen but all evidence of her brother was long gone.

'I don't know. I lost them.'

'Really? Thank God it's not just me who gets lost. If I hadn't seen you through the window I think I'd have been wandering round this horrible place for the rest of my life.'

'Sorry about before.' I forced myself not to think about Rhys. Thinking about him, even for a millisecond made me wanted to cry. Tears were very close, I could feel them gathering behind my eyes but there was no way I was going to let them out.

'I'm sorry, too.'

We both smiled. It didn't make me feel any better, though. Looking at Hannah only reminded me of him even more.

'Please tell me you know how to get to the place where we're supposed to meet the coach?'

'Not really. But I'm sure we can find it.' I picked up my bag. I wanted to get a million miles away from the computer.

Neither of us said much as we tried to find familiar landmarks. Hannah had something on her mind. For a split second I wondered if she'd been watching me through the window of the Internet café and knew I'd been mailing Rhys. But that was just crazy. She couldn't have seen that far from outside.

And even Hannah with all her belief in fate, destiny, tarot cards and psychic ability couldn't read minds. Not that it would matter now if she could. Rhys had obviously made a decision. He wasn't interested in me. He'd probably found someone else, Olivia or some other girl from college. There were enough of them to choose from and they were always flirting with him. Why should he keep turning them down? We all knew what lads his age were like. They thought about sex all the time. Needed to have sex on a regular basis. He wasn't getting that with me and wasn't likely to either. By the law of averages there'd be someone at college he'd fancy eventually.

I had to turn away and pretend to blow my nose. I fought the tears away.

'You're not getting a cold are you?' Hannah was concerned, which made me feel much worse.

'No. I don't think so.' I was in control again. 'Come on. I think it's this way.'

I headed off down a street that looked sort of familiar. Every person we passed seemed to be part of a couple. Everywhere I looked people were holding hands, laughing and joking. Everyone was happy apart from me. Back in Hollyoaks Rhys was probably with his other woman right now. He'd probably been with her when I IMed him and that's why he'd signed off in such a hurry. Anger started to burn in the pit of my stomach. It's the same feeling I get in a swim race when I do a bad turn or fluff a stroke and get behind, but know I'm much better than the people ahead of me. Then I use that anger. My stroke quickens, my legs get stronger and the only thing I'm focused on is catching the other swimmers up, catching them up and passing them. I forget how much my lungs are burning, I don't think about the pain I'll be in at the end of the race. All I think about is beating the other people.

If Rhys didn't want me, then fine. If Rhys had found someone else, then that was fine, too. But two could play at that game.

Nancy and Murphy were already sitting on a wall in the park waiting for the coach when we arrived. A few of the others were there, too, but no sign of the teachers. As we walked up, Nancy and Murphy were sitting close, deep in conversation. I thought for a moment his hand was brushing her leg, but it must have been my imagination. As soon as she saw us Nancy leapt up and ran over.

'Where have you two been?' She couldn't stop grinning. 'You should see all the stuff we've collected. We're bound to win.'

She held out the plastic bag that was crammed with all our C items. I was just glad she didn't mention my storming off. I'd really wanted to win at the start of the day, but all that seemed pointless now.

Half-heartedly, Hannah and I peered into the bag. A really horrible smell wafted out and we both recoiled backwards.

'It stinks.' Hannah wrinkled her nose. 'What have you got in there?'

'That'll be the Chaource.' Murphy came up to join us. He looked at me and smiled.

'Which is?' Hannah tried to have another whiff but didn't even get close.

'Local cheese. We wangled a free sample. I think they just wanted rid of it cos it smelt so bad.' Nancy closed the bag, but the cheesy smell still lingered.

'Murphy's law says that it begins with C for cheese and C for the type of cheese,' Murphy said, 'so I reckon it counts as two for our team.'

'Or none.'

We'd been so busy being knocked out by the smell of the cheese that none of us had noticed Stacy and the chavettes walk up to us. She ripped the bag out of Nancy's hand and started to back away from us, swinging it round over her head.

'Give that back,' Nancy yelled. We all went after her.

'Yeah. Give it back Stacy. Don't be such a bitch.' Murphy leapt forward and tried to grab the bag. Stacy skipped out of reach.

'Why not? You think I'm a bitch whatever I do.'

'No I don't.'

Stacy headed further into the park. There was a lake to her left, home to lots of ducks being fed by small children.

'I think you're a psychotic freak,' Murphy finished. 'Why do you think I dumped you?'

It wasn't the best thing to say to someone who was holding something of yours to ransom. She swung the bag faster and faster above her head and then, as it swung in the direction of the lake, she let go. We all watched it fly through the air. It was like the world had gone into slow motion. The bag made a graceful arc as it headed out over the water and it chose that moment to open up. Like some weird bag-shaped cloud the letter C items – the cigar, the coffee cup, the cap and the candle – started raining out and dropping into the water, sending the ducks into a panic. Finally, the bag itself hit the water and bobbed up and down like a capsized boat.

Stacy and the chavettes ran back out of the

park laughing, but we just stood there, in complete shock. Everything we'd worked so hard for, or not so hard for in some cases, was gone, sunk to the bottom or being pecked at by the ducks or floating away across the lake.

Hannah shrugged and cradled her shopping bag to her chest.

'At least I've still got my shoes.' She suddenly grinned and started to laugh. And we all joined in. It was impossible not to. The scavenger hunt didn't matter. Stacy didn't matter.

Behind us the bus pulled up and we all turned to head back towards it. I hung back and grabbed Murphy's arm. Nancy and Hannah linked arms in front. I waited until they were just out of earshot.

'You still want to go to the cinema tonight?' I asked.

He gave me a weird look, glanced at Hannah and Nancy, then back at me.

'What's changed your mind?' he asked.

'Dunno. I just think it'd be a laugh.'

He looked thoughtful for a moment.

'How do I know you're still not pining for this secret boyfriend and just using me?'

'You'll have to take my word for it.'

'OK. Your word is more than good enough for me. But better not rub Stacy's nose in it any more than we have to. I'll meet you outside the cinema about 7.15ish?'

I nodded and smiled.

'We'd better catch the others up.' He jogged towards them and I followed. The anger still burned right in the pit of my stomach, but I felt much better.

Hannah

Back on the coach, Mr Lang wasn't impressed when Nancy told him that we'd lost our collection of C things. He didn't seem to believe our story of having left the bag in a café and that by the time we remembered and went back it had gone. I mean, it was pretty hard to believe. Why would anyone take a bag full of rubbish? But despite us all hating Stacy not one of us was prepared to grass her up. It was the unwritten rule. Though I often think that the person who wrote that rule must have been one of the bullies who didn't want to be grassed up.

The prize for the winning team was only a box of Belgium chocolates anyway, those ones that look like shells. Stacy's team didn't win either, which made it slightly better. In the end Beaky's team won for having collected the most things and the prize for the most ingenious item went to a team from the other school. They'd been given the letter K and had come back with a piece of paper covered in lipstick kisses. They said that they'd gone round the town asking any lipstick-wearing women they came across to plant a kiss on the paper and autograph it. It was a pretty neat idea. At first, I'd thought that Mr Lang and Miss O'Donnell liked it because the team would have had to talk in French to lots of different people, which meant they'd used lots of initiative. But then Nancy leant over and whispered to us that her and Murphy had seen the two teachers kissing and that made much more sense. They liked it because it was romantic and that's why I liked it too, I had romantic thoughts on the brain. Tonight might be the night that changed my life forever. The night my soulmate and I would speak for the first time. I started smiling to myself as a little shiver shot up my spine. I'd decided to say nothing to the others. They'd only want to come with me and I knew this was something I had to do on my own. We'd already planned to go into the village that evening. I'd make up an excuse about feeling tired or having a headache and pretend to go back to the château. Then I'd sneak into the same café we'd seen him in the night before and that's when the magic would happen.

No one said much on the way back to the

château. We all seemed to be deep in thought. I was planning my outfit. I'd got the perfect shoes and a new top, exactly like one I'd seen Keira Knightley wear except without the huge price tag. I already knew which skirt would go perfectly with it. I closed my eyes and rested my head back against the seat. Tonight was going to be amazing. I had such a good feeling about it. I banished any tiny morsel of negative thought from my head. Nothing would go wrong; it was the power of positive thought.

Nancy

I was glad no one wanted to talk on the way back to the château. It meant I could concentrate on thinking about Murphy and what might happen that evening at the cinema. From where I was sitting, if I craned my neck a little and tilted my head to one side, I could just see the top of his head further down the coach. I smiled, reliving the moment he asked me out. How cool was that? He actually asked me out. I wondered if we'd kiss each other. If I had anything to do with it we would. I bet he was an amazing kisser, better than Justin Burton any day.

It even felt amazing when Murphy was just touching me or standing close. The chemistry was electric. I wouldn't sleep with him though, not until I knew we were going to have a relationship. He didn't seem like the sort of guy who would be into one-night stands, anyway. Though one of my ten rules about boys was that every member of the male species would be into one-night stands if they got the chance. But Murphy was different and even if he asked I wouldn't think any less of him. If things went really well, I could move back in with my parents and be much closer to him. We could even end up going to the same university together. That would be cool. All the other girls would either envy me or want to be me.

OK, maybe I was thinking ahead a little bit too far. I didn't want to turn into Hannah. It was exciting, though. All I had to do was figure out how to get away from the others when we went into the village that evening. I could just make up some excuse and say I was going back to the château. I could fake illness or just say I was tired. I'd think of something. I'd slip away and go and meet Murphy and no one would have a clue.

Sarah

I spent the whole of the journey back to the château staring out of the window. I should have been looking forward to seeing Murphy later on.

He was a great guy. Good looking, funny and sweet. Any girl would be dead chuffed to be going out with him. In fact I was lucky. As Nancy and Hannah had told me he really really liked me. How many guys did I meet that fell head over heels for me? I couldn't not have a great time with him.

If that was true why did I feel so down? I watched three raindrops trickle down the glass until they merged into one. It was a game I'd played with Rhys. We'd been round at his house. I'd gone round to visit Hannah knowing she wouldn't be there. We stayed and chatted all day. It was amazing. He'd gone through his record collection with me – I hadn't heard of most of the bands, of course; they'd all had weird names like Beulah, Flaming Lips, The Decemberists – and then he'd chosen his favourite CD of the moment, something by a band called Wilco, and we'd sat on his bed and listened to it. It had been raining outside and as we'd listened to the music he'd told me to pick a raindrop. He picked one too and we watched as they raced down the glass together. 'First one to the bottom wins,' he'd said. My raindrop had won, but when I asked what my prize was he just smiled and his cheeks flushed a little.

I shook myself. I had to stop thinking about him. He didn't want me. I had to push him right out of my mind, store all my memories of him in that little room and never let them out. Otherwise I would end up old and alone. Nancy was right: you had to grab what you could from life when you got the chance. Like going out with Murphy. I would have a good time. I was determined. Sod Rhys. If he didn't need me, then I didn't need him either.

Hannah

It was just after 6.30pm when we sat in a booth at one of the cafes in the village. It was a weird atmosphere, no one in a talkative mood.

'Are you two still annoyed at me for stomping off this morning?' I asked, certain that was the reason for their silence.

'No.' Sarah looked at me in surprise.

'Of course not. Why would you think that?' Nancy also looked taken aback.

'It's just that everyone's so quiet.'

'Are we?' Sarah shrugged, 'Sorry.'

'Actually, I'm feeling a bit sick.' Nancy pulled a pained face. 'Think I might have a migraine coming on.'

'I didn't know you got migraines.' I looked at her. She didn't look sick. In fact, she looked great. She'd done her eyes just like a fifties movie star and was wearing a dress I'd never seen before.

'I do occasionally. I start seeing stars and

feeling sick. Half an hour later I get a really bad pain in the side of my head. It's horrible. The only thing I can do is lay down in a darkened room until it goes.'

'Sounds horrible.' Sarah looked at her sympathetically.

'It is.' Nancy got up. 'I'll have to go back to the château. You don't mind, do you?'

'Of course not. Do you want us to come with you?' Sarah started to get up.

'No,' Nancy snapped back. She took a breath and calmed herself, 'No point in all our nights being ruined. Anyway, best thing for me is to be in our room on my own.'

Sarah sat back down.

'OK. As long as you're sure.'

'Positive. You stay. I'll be fine.' She smiled weakly and headed out of the door.

'I feel bad we didn't go with her,' Sarah said, after she'd gone.

'You heard her. She wants to be on her own.' I felt bad, but I wasn't going to miss out on what might be my last opportunity to talk to Mr Mysterious. But it did make it much more difficult to get away from Sarah.

'I suppose.' Sarah glanced at her watch.

'And we don't want her to be ill for tomorrow.' Sarah brightened up.

'We're still going then?'

'Course. It'll be so cool. Wandering down the Champs Élysées. Seeing the Eiffel Tower. It's the romantic capital of the world.'

'It's only romantic if you're with the man you love.' She looked really sad when she said that. She had a point, but I wasn't going to let anything get me down. Not tonight. No negative thoughts were allowed.

'Don't you want to see Notre Dame? Montmartre?'

'Mum and Dad went for a weekend last year. She said it was too crowded and the people were really rude.'

'What is wrong with you tonight?' I didn't want her negative thoughts rubbing off on me.

'Nothing.' She looked at her watch again. It was about the tenth time since we'd sat down.

'Am I keeping you?'

She gave me a funny look.

'No. It's just that I . . . erm . . . I promised Mum I'd email her about training. Let her know my times and stuff. And if I don't she'll probably ring the school to find out what's happened.' She hesitated. I could tell she was feeling guilty, 'In fact I think I'll go and do it now.'

She got up.

'You don't mind, do you?'

On any other night I would have minded a whole lot. Who wants to be a Bridget Jones wannabe, sitting on her own looking like she's been stood up? But tonight it was absolutely perfect.

'No. You go.' I smiled to let her know it really was OK.

'Sure? What will you do?'

'I'll probably have another coffee. See if I can find some of the others. You go. It's fine.'

She gave me one last look, then smiled and left.

I waited for five minutes, the longest five minutes of my life, before I left too, via the loos.

I checked my reflection in the mirror and reapplied my lipstick. I was pleased with the person looking back at me. My stomach was fizzing with excitement and nerves. I didn't even allow myself to think about him not being there. I just knew that he would be. Fate had waved her magic wand. Nothing could stop me now.

I stepped into Le Café des Amis. It was busy. I noticed a few people from the château were already there. I scanned the room. No sign of Mr Mysterious but he was there, somewhere, I could feel it. I stepped further into the room. Then, suddenly, horror. Out of the corner of my eye I noticed Beaky. He'd seen me and he was walking in my direction. He wasn't in my plans. It was all going to go wrong. I turned to get away from him and then, so close to me that I could almost touch him, there was Mr Mysterious. He was standing head turned slightly away from me. He looked as gorgeous as he'd done the night before. And for one moment I froze. Like in some horrible nightmare my feet were stuck to the floor. Mr Mysterious within my grasp, Beaky rapidly approaching from the other direction and I froze. He was just so perfect. Standing so close I could see his beautiful eyelashes, so long most girls would kill to have them, and his perfectly pouting lips.

I yanked myself back to the real world. I could do this. I was going to do this. I took another step forward and opened my mouth to introduce myself. The rest of the room faded into the background. There was just him and me. My hand was almost on his shoulder, the words already forming in my throat.

And then he started to smile and hold his own hands out. But he wasn't looking at me. I followed his gaze. One of Stacy's chavette mates was there and she was smiling back at him. He whispered the words, 'Bonsoir, chérie, t'es belle ce soir', gathered her up in his arms and kissed her. She melted and they became entangled like there was no one else in the room. The words I was about to say to him, the words I'd practised over and over, died on my tongue. I stood and watched them, and felt my heart breaking into a million pieces because I knew that could have been me. If only I hadn't waited. If only I'd grabbed my chance when it was there in front of me.

I turned and ran out of the door, pushing my way past Beaky as he said something that I couldn't understand. And as soon as I hit the fresh air I burst into tears. I didn't stop running until I got back to the château. I went straight to our room, barely even noticed that Nancy wasn't there, threw myself down on to the bed and yelled my heart out.

Nancy

I felt bad lying to Hannah and Sarah, though not that bad. Sarah lied to Hannah every time she didn't tell her about Rhys. And Sarah hadn't been interested in Murphy anyway, so she had no reason to be upset. OK, so it was pretty twisted logic, but as long as I kept repeating it to myself I could live with it.

I got to the cinema at ten to seven. I didn't want to look like I was that bothered so I hid down an alleyway. I could see the front of the cinema from where I was standing, but no one could see me. I hoped so, anyway. It got to one minute to seven. I was checking my watch like a maniac as well as looking up at the clock on the spire of the building next to the cinema.

Time crept on. Seven o'clock came and went. Then five past, then ten past. My heart started to shrivel. He wasn't coming. I'd been kidding myself. It had just been one big joke. Him and his mates were probably having a right laugh about it. Why did I think he'd want to go out with me anyway? Not weird, kooky Nancy. Why would someone as fit and cool and popular as him want to go out with me?

As the hands of the clock were about to click to twenty past, and I was about to drag myself back to the château and spinsterdom, a movement across the street stopped me leaving. I looked over and there he was. He appeared from the street next to the cinema, walked right up to the front of the building, looked round and then shoved his hands in his pocket. My heart leapt. He was here. He really had turned up. I was going to get to go on a date with him.

I wanted to sprint across the street, yelling and laughing, but I made myself saunter as casually as if it was half past six. He saw me coming and smiled. I don't want to brag but his whole face lit up.

'Thought you'd stood me up.'

'Sorry. Girl's prerogative to be late.'

'You're here, now. And looking gorgeous.' He took a long look at me. I felt a shiver go down my back and I was certain I was grinning like an idiot. I must stay cool.

'You want to go in?' I asked, thinking ahead to sitting at the back of a dark cinema, cuddled up right next to him.

'Do you mind if we wait a few minutes?'

'Why?' I didn't care. I was still grinning like an idiot.

'Because I want to do this.' He leant forward and kissed me. It was the most incredible thing. He kissed me and kept kissing. I thought my legs were going to give way beneath me so I put my arms around him and clung to him. I hoped he couldn't hear my heart thundering and I hoped he was thinking the same about me as I was about him.

'Nancy?' A disembodied and confused sounding voice drifted into my ear. Suddenly, Murphy wasn't kissing me any more. He pushed me away and turned his head. My legs were still wobbly. I wasn't sure what was happening.

'What the . . . ?' That voice again. It sounded familiar. 'But I thought . . . you said . . . we were . . .' The voice stopped. Whoever it was sounded in pain. I turned to see where it was coming from and there, standing almost within arm's reach, was Sarah. The look on her face was awful.

'Hi, Sarah. Glad you could make it,' Murphy seemed to be saying. I looked at him and he was smiling at her. What was he talking about?

'You were kissing her?' Sarah sounded close to tears.

'I know. Jealous?' Murphy stepped towards her. She kept looking at me like I'd got two heads or something, and then at him.

A horrible awful feeling started to gnaw away in my stomach.

'I thought you liked me?' she asked. And then I knew.

'I do. But I wasn't sure if you were serious about me. I didn't even know if you'd turn up tonight. You've been giving me the run around since we arrived. Flirting one minute, ignoring me the next.'

'What about me?' I blurted, even though I already knew what he would say.

'You're a laugh.' He shrugged. 'A good backup. You knew that, though.' He laughed. 'You've been trying to set me and Sarah up all week.'

Sarah looked at me.

'You said you had a headache.'

'I know.'

'And all the time you were planning on meeting him?'

I wanted the ground to open up and some great big troll-like monster to grab my feet and drag me away just so I wouldn't have to look at Sarah's face.

'You told me I should go out with him. You practically shoved us together.'

'I'm sorry. I thought you weren't interested.'

'So you thought you'd stick your tongue down his throat instead?' She paused, and then her face grew even darker, 'You planned this, didn't you? You knew I'd be here. You knew I'd see you together. You did this on purpose. You wanted to make me look stupid.'

Then she really lost it. Murphy looked completely out of his depth. He would have legged it if he could have done it and not looked like a complete coward.

'Is this all still because of Rhys? You're jealous of me and him.'

'No . . . I didn't know you were meeting him.'

She started shouting. A bunch of people from our school and Murphy's school came walking past and stopped to watch.

'I don't believe you. You're just a horrible, evil cow. You've never liked me. I told myself it was my imagination. But it's not. You really do, you really hate me. Why? What have I ever done to you?'

'I don't hate you.'

'Ever since you started at school you've done everything you possibly could to leave me out, always making bitchy comments, trying to make me look stupid and feel like I wasn't good enough. Have you any idea how many times I've gone home and cried because you'd been so horrible to me? When I said you were a bully the other night, I lied when I said I didn't mean it. You're a horrible, vicious, pathetic bully. Worse than Stacy. Worse than anyone.'

'I'm not the only one who's done horrible things. You three ganged up on me after Christmas and, even when I told you that I'd made a mistake snogging Justin, you still took Nicole's side. You pretended to be my friend just to humiliate me. How d'you think that made me feel?'

'Well, you've got me back now, haven't you? I hope you're happy.'

'Yeah. I'm over the moon. I tried my best to get you to go out with Murphy and you threw it back in my face. You can't blame me for taking my chance with him.'

'You're a real bitch, you know that?'

'And you're the one lying to your best friend and sneaking around with her brother. Nothing gets lower than that.'

'Whatever I do, I'll never be lower than you. You're selfish and nasty and then you wonder why people are always falling out with you. You don't deserve any friends. I hope you die sad and alone.'

I thought for a moment she was going to slap me. She raised her hand but saw the crowd watching and turned and ran.

I stood there. She might not have touched me, but I felt like I'd been slapped. It was horrible. Murphy looked at me.

'You really are a bitch, aren't you?' he said, and then turned and walked away. I can truly and honestly say that it was one of the worst moments of my entire life. At that moment I had nothing. I knew Sarah would run to Hannah and tell her everything. Hannah would take her side and I'd be the one completely in the wrong. OK, I was partly in the wrong, but not completely. My only argument back would be to tell Hannah about Sarah and Rhys, but I couldn't do that. I'd promised I wouldn't. And by the time Sarah had finished telling her what a total bitch I was I wasn't sure Hannah would believe me anyway. If Sarah denied it, Hannah would believe her over me every single time. But why shouldn't she? I was everything Sarah said. I did hurt people, sometimes by accident – like now – but sometimes on purpose. If I was hurting, then making someone else feel as bad as me seemed to help. For a little bit, anyway. But I had no idea that Sarah had been hurt so much, and it was all down to me. I had no idea I had that effect on people. It's not how I wanted to be.

I was totally alone. I'd messed everything up. I couldn't even start to think about Murphy and how I'd, just for those few moments, really believed he was interested in me. That feeling of incredible happiness had now been torn to shreds. I wanted to curl up in a little ball and cry. I hated Murphy. I hated Sarah. And I hated the world for always, always ganging up on me. But most of all I hated myself.

I had nowhere to go so I wandered round and round the village. I never wanted to face Hannah or Sarah again.

Sarah

Seeing Murphy and Nancy kissing made me feel sick. At first I didn't even realize what I was seeing. I thought it was some sort of joke. But the way they were, the way they didn't stop for what seemed like forever and the look on Nancy's face when she saw me standing there, told me it wasn't a joke.

It was like being punched in the stomach. As I stumbled back to the château the scene kept replaying over and over in my head. The things that Murphy said, the look on his face. Had I really been flirting with him? I'd been friendly with him, but nothing more, or so I thought.

Then there was Nancy staring at me like she'd won the big prize. She'd probably been planning this all along, in fact probably ever since that time just after Christmas when we had all fallen out with her. But that had been her fault. She snogged Justin knowing that Nicole was still in love with him. You just don't betray your friends like that. Of course, now I'd betrayed Rhys and for what? Just to be publicly humiliated. If Rhys ever found out that would be it for us, not that there was an 'us'. I started to cry as I walked along.

I went into our room and even before I stepped through the door I could hear someone crying. For one horrible moment I thought it was Nancy, but I knew she couldn't have got back before me. And what had she got to cry about anyway? I stepped inside and saw Hannah lying on her bad surrounded by crumpled tissues. James Blunt was playing on the stereo. Seems like he made everyone miserable.

'What's wrong?' I sat down next to her. I thought something really awful must have happened, some terrible news from home.

She sat up and blew her nose.

'I'm sorry. I didn't tell you, but I had to do it on my own because I thought you'd laugh at me if I chickened out. But I didn't.' Her voice was trembling and it was hard to make any sense of what she was saying.

'What?'

'I went to find Mr Mysterious and he was there and he looked beautiful and I had rehearsed everything I was going to say. I was going to be assertive, grab the opportunity, just like Nancy said. And I was about to touch him, say hello and then from nowhere one of Stacy's stupid chav mates jumped into his arms and snogged his face off . . . right in front of me. It was the most horrible thing I've ever seen.'

'Oh, my God. What did you do?'

'I ran. What am I going to do? My whole life is a disaster.' She looked at me and her whole face crumpled again. I couldn't help it. I started crying too and we hugged and cried and hugged again until eventually Hannah pulled away and looked at me.

'I've been so into my own problems I haven't even asked you how it went with your Mum? Did you email her?'

'It's awful, Hannah. I lied to you too. I didn't come back here to email Mum. I had a date with Murphy.'

'Really? Oh . . . Really? How did it go?'

'Terrible. When I got there he was kissing Nancy.'

'What? Nancy and Murphy?'

I nodded.

'She did it on purpose just to get at me. She really hates me Han . . . she's never forgiven me for us falling out at Christmas. It was so horrible. There was a crowd watching. I've never felt so humiliated.'

'This doesn't make sense. Are you sure?'

'It was all planned. She denied it, but I could tell she was lying. Murphy said as much. He said I'd led him on and that's why they'd done this. Just to punish me. Am I that awful a person?'

'No, of course you're not. You're lovely.'

'I bet she doesn't even fancy him. She just didn't want me to have him. I thought we were friends. How could she do this to me?'

Hannah's face changed. Her chin jutted out and her eyes started to burn with anger. I knew she was on my side. Her own miserable evening was pushed to one side.

'Because she's a bitch. I thought she was acting weird with Murphy today. Flirting with him. Giving him looks when she thought I wasn't watching.'

'Really?'

'I didn't say anything because I thought you weren't interested in him. What made you change your mind? And why didn't you tell me?'

I blinked at her. I couldn't tell her the real reason I'd changed my mind.

'I, erm . . . just thought . . . holiday's nearly over . . . why not take a chance . . .' I stumbled over the words.

'Like me with Mr Mysterious.'

'And I didn't tell you because I wasn't sure I'd go through with it.'

'Exactly the same with me.' She smiled. 'We're like twins.'

We hugged again. I was so glad to have a friend like Hannah. She'd never stab me in the back. A pang of guilt hit me like a slap round the face. She was such a good friend to me and there I was lying to her about Rhys. But I was so mad at Nancy I didn't care that I knew she was probably hurting as bad as me and that she was right about Rhys. Now I didn't have Rhys and I didn't have Murphy either. The thought of Rhys made me cry again, which set Hannah off again. We both bawled like little kids for at least half an hour.

'I wish I never had to see Nancy again,' I said when we eventually stopped crying.

'It's her who should be wanting to hide away.' Hannah started tidying the room.

'But she'll be back soon. What am I going to say to her?'

'You don't have to say anything. In fact, we'll both just ignore her. Show her that she can't go round doing things like that.'

'What about Paris?'

Hannah stopped tidying and sat back on the bed.

'I'm not going if she's going and we can't go without her. It was her idea.' I sighed. One more thing Nancy had spoiled for us.

'We're still going. She can do what she likes, but she's not coming with us.'

'Just you and me? Can we do that?'

'We don't need Nancy. Why can't we do it? All we have to do is buy a train ticket. It's not difficult. We have to go.'

'We do?'

'Yeah, because Nancy will assume that if she doesn't go we'll chicken out. She thinks we can't do stuff like that without her. That she's the only one who can be the rebel. Well, she's wrong. We're going to Paris.' When Hannah made her mind up, there was no one more determined, 'What d'you think?'

'I think you're right. We can do this without her. In fact I can't wait to see her face when she realizes we're still going. Serve her right.'

Hannah grinned at me and I grinned back. I wondered if Hannah was as nervous as me about going to Paris on our own. She didn't look it. But we did have something to prove to Nancy so, however scary it was, we'd do it. Like Hannah said, all we had to do was go the train station in the village, buy tickets and sit on the train until it got to Paris. What could go wrong?

Nancy

I was cold and my feet were starting to ache. I sat for ages on a bench outside the château, shivering and wondering what Sarah and Hannah were talking about. I didn't have to wonder too much. It was pretty obvious.

I waited as long as I could, hoping they might have fallen asleep, before I went inside. I crept up to our door and stood outside for a few moments. I strained my ears but I couldn't hear anything. Maybe they were asleep?

I opened the door as quietly as I could and stepped in. The bedside lights were still on and my heart sank as I saw them sitting together on Sarah's bed. They didn't look up as I came in.

'We're going to have a great time tomorrow.' Hannah said to Sarah, but it was obvious it was for my benefit. I realized they must be talking about the Paris trip. I'd forgotten all about it until that moment. Going to Paris was the last thing on my mind.

'I know. What time do you think we should set off?' Sarah asked. They were blanking me.

'Early. It'll be fab, won't it? Just the two of us. We'll have the best time ever.'

Fine. They wanted to go without me, see if I cared.

'I'm totally excited.' Hannah climbed into her bed but kept her back to me. I might as well not have existed.

'And thank God a certain person won't be there to spoil things.' Sarah got into her own bed. They lay facing each other.

'We don't want that spiteful cow anywhere near us.' Hannah said, with so much venom in her voice it really hurt.

'You haven't even heard my side of the story.' I couldn't stop myself.

'Did you hear something, Sarah?' Hannah gazed around the room.

'I don't think so. Maybe it was someone next door.'

'Probably. Annoying though.'

'How childish?' I felt hot tears stab at my eyes, 'I haven't done anything wrong. This is totally unfair.'

'There it goes again,' Sarah said.

'We should complain.' Hannah pulled her duvet up further to her ear.

'It isn't my fault Murphy asked us both out. I didn't know. He messed us both around.' I wanted to shake them both. Make them see.

'Or buy some ear plugs. Still, we won't have this problem tomorrow.' Sarah plumped her pillows and flopped back down.

'Thank God.' Hannah turned out her light.

'Why am I getting all the blame? I'm not the only one who's done things wrong. You're not being fair.'

'Night, Han.'

'Night, Sarah.'

Sarah flicked her light off, leaving me in darkness.

'Fine. Like I care anyway. Go to Paris. Whatever. And if you want to believe what Sarah says, Hannah, then go ahead. She knows what's really going on here . . . pity she's too scared to be really honest with you.'

I turned on my bedside light, grabbed my make-up bag and ran for the bathroom. It was only then, locked in a cubicle, that I burst into tears.

Paris and Being Saved

WEDNESDAY

Hannah

'You ask. Your French is better than mine.' I pushed Sarah towards the ticket office in the train station.

She gave me a look but stepped up to the window.

'Erm . . . hi . . . *bonjour*, I mean. Erm . . . *deux billets* to, erm . . . Paris. Thanks.'

The man behind the window raised his eyebrows.

'Is that wrong?' Sarah turned to look at me.

'No. Your French was perfect.' The ticket man winked at me and started tapping away at his machine, '*Aller ou aller-retour?*' He started to laugh.

'*Retournez*,' I said over Sarah's shoulder.

Sarah grinned at me. She looked as excited as I felt. We'd sneaked out of the château leaving Nancy fast asleep in bed. It was fun tiptoeing down the corridor doing the comedy cartoon walk. The hardest part was trying not to laugh. Neither of us mentioned the night before.

We hadn't had to wait long for the train – apparently French trains always turn up on time – and even better it had a Paris sign in big LED letters on the front. No danger of getting on the wrong train. We'd even got a carriage all to ourselves.

'I told you we didn't need Nancy.'

'It's been pretty easy so far.' Sarah nodded in agreement. She was starting to look miserable again, though. I wondered if she was thinking about Murphy.

'Dead easy. Practically everyone in France speaks English now, anyway. And when we get to Paris we'll just jump in a taxi and ask them to take us straight to the Champs Élysées.' I smiled to try and cheer her up.

'I wonder what she's doing now.'

'Who?'

'Nancy.' Sarah sounded like she almost felt sorry for her.

'Who cares?'

'I know . . . but . . .'

'She brought this on herself. What she did to you was unforgivable. And it's not the first time she's done something like that, either.' And if Nancy hadn't gone on at me I would never even have thought about going back to find Mr Mysterious. Everything that had gone wrong on our holiday was her fault.

'I suppose.'

'I bet she doesn't even know we've gone yet. She'll still be asleep.'

The train pulled into another station. A twenty-something guy listening to music on his headphones and a really ancient man carrying a cat in a carrier settled into seats at the opposite end of the carriage.

'Are you OK, Sarah? We could always get off and catch the next train back.'

'No. I'm glad we decided to come.'

'Me, too. Better than a day of boring bike riding and orienteering.'

'That's true.'

'And maybe it'll teach Nancy a lesson.' I wasn't sure what lesson, but in movies people learn stuff all the time. Like how to be a better person.

'Maybe. I hope she doesn't get any grief off Stacy and her mates.'

I hadn't thought about that. The news of Nancy kissing Murphy would be all round the château by now. When Stacy found out she'd probably go ballistic. Even Nancy wasn't a match for a four-against-one contest.

'She can look after herself,' I said, but with more confidence than I felt.

'Yeah.' Sarah didn't sound convinced either.

'Should we listen to some music?' I got out my MP3 player. I didn't want to think about Nancy. We shared the headphones, one earpiece each, and listened to Robbie's latest album. Some excitement returned, but I still had a bad feeling in my stomach. Even when she wasn't around Nancy was still spoiling our fun.

Nancy

It took ages for me to get to sleep, that night. Every time I closed my eyes I could see Sarah's shocked face and Murphy, sneering down his nose, saying 'You're all right for a laugh.' I had to screw my face up to stop myself from crying.

I wasn't going to give the others the satisfaction, but all I wanted to do was ring Becca and bawl my eyes out. I wished I could click my fingers and wake up in my own bed. Becca would know what to do. She'd understand. I could tell her everything, even about Sarah and Rhys. That's the great thing about having an older sister. You don't keep secrets from each other; well, Becca and me don't anyway. With a big sister you can tell them anything and not worry about them going behind your back and telling someone else. I wanted to be home so badly.

When I did fall asleep I had a horrible nightmare that I woke up in the château and everyone had gone back to England and left me behind. I was running up and down the corridors looking for someone. Finally, I went into the kitchen. Miss Rousseau was in there with Becca. I couldn't understand what they were doing. I asked Becca to help me but she just smiled, and then I noticed she was holding Miss Rousseau's hand. They started to lean towards each other and I knew they were going to kiss. I woke up with a start and didn't go back to sleep.

About an hour or so later, Sarah and Hannah got up and spent the next hour whispering to each other as they got ready. I squeezed my eyes tight shut. I didn't want them to know I was awake.

After they'd gone I lay staring at the ceiling. Was this what Hannah meant when she went on about karma? I'm quite willing to admit that I'd started lots of arguments in the past, stirred things up sometimes, and I'll even admit that I can be a little bitchy. I prefer feisty, but my feisty seems to be other people's bitchy. So here I was, excommunicated from my friends for something I didn't do or rather something I didn't know I was doing. I was an innocent party. Maybe I shouldn't have said yes to Murphy, but he asked and he's gorgeous and Sarah was in love with someone else. It's all totally unfair.

I replayed the events over and over. At first it just made me cry or would have done if I did the crying thing. All the crying went on inside me as I curled up and dug my fingernails into my palms to stop the tears sneaking out. But after a while I started to get angry. I'd done nothing wrong and Murphy had been hideous to me. First, I was mad at him. Then, when I'd imagined all the horrible things that could happen to him – flesh-eating bugs, six-foot-long tape worms, those Amazon insects that crawl up your bum and suck your blood before exploding out through your skin (Jake loves watching documentaries like that on the Discovery Channel) – I moved on to Sarah. How ungrateful was she? I'd been trying to help her since we arrived and she'd chucked it all back in my face. Then she goes and changes her mind without telling me, and somehow it's my fault. She needs to get a life. Finally, I vented my fury at Hannah. She made me the angriest. That she believed Sarah's story straight away without waiting to hear my side. How fair was that? Sarah says one thing bad about me and Hannah buys it. I'm trying to protect her from finding out about Rhys and that's how she repays me. Of course, she doesn't know I'm protecting her, but if she ever finds out she's going to feel really bad.

I heard everyone else coming and going down the hallway outside. Miss Rousseau shouting at Stacy and her mates. Normally hearing them get yelled at would make me feel better but I didn't care about them any more.

I waited until everything went quiet, then I got up and slowly got ready. I didn't want to see or speak to anyone. I didn't want to do any activities. All I wanted was to be on my own.

I took my last stash of Pringles and Coke and wandered down to the lake. I took the long route so no one would see me, but the place was deserted anyway. For a millisecond I thought maybe my nightmare had come true, but then I reminded myself it was just a stupid dream.

It was a beautiful day that totally didn't fit with my mood. I wanted a drab, grey winter's day that reminded me of tortured Victorian heroines and tragic endings, not this happy, blue sky of spring, where the sun was warm and all the birds fluttered and sang like they'd just won the *X-Factor* and been complimented by Simon Cowell.

I sat on one of the seats and looked out across

the lake back towards the château. Sarah and Hannah would probably be in Paris by now, having a great time and thinking how much better off they were without me.

To distract myself I opened the Pringles, but I wasn't hungry. A bunch of ducks and swans glided up. I had no idea how they heard the pop of Pringles being opened. I mean, it's not like birds have great big ears that stick out the side of their heads. I guess sticky-out ears would make flying a little difficult. But however they do it birds always seem to know when food's around. I decided to throw a couple of Pringles in their direction, seeing as they'd made the effort. Have you ever tried to throw a Pringle? It doesn't work. They get stuck in the air and go about ten centimetres before fluttering back in your direction and landing closer than if you'd leant forward and put it on the ground by hand. I tried three times. Each time the Pringle landed closer to me. The harder I threw the worse the result. The ducks and swans paddled in front of me and I swear they were laughing at how pathetic I was.

'Well, come here then if you want one so badly,' I snapped at them. The biggest, meanest looking swan sort of cocked his head at me and swam in a circle.

'Who doesn't like Pringles? You or the birds?'

Startled, I looked round. Miss Rousseau was standing a little way behind me. I wondered how long she'd been there.

She stepped forward.

'Can I join you?'

I nodded, and moved my rucksack to make space for her. She sat down, but didn't say anything for a while. Then she took a deep breath and exhaled slowly.

'This is my favourite place in the whole park. I love the way the lake reflects the château, it makes it look like it's not real. A fairy-tale castle.'

'That's what Hannah said when we arrived. That it looked like something from a fairy tale.'

'She's a romantic, your friend?'

'Yeah,' I replied. I must have sounded very gloomy because it made Miss Rousseau look at me.

'But no fairy tale for you?'

'Don't believe in them.'

'The monsters and the heroes?'

'And the happy endings.' She sighed, and looked back at the lake.

'Did you know that swans mate for life? Once they find a partner, their love lasts forever.'

'Birds can't fall in love,' I scoffed. 'And nothing lasts forever.'

'In the swan's world it does. Even if their mate

dies it's very rare for them to find a new mate. They live the rest of their life alone.'

I looked at her to see if she was messing me about, but her face was totally serious.

'That's really sad.'

'But beautiful too, no?'

'Pity human beings can't be like that.'

'Some can. Just knowing it's possible is enough.'

'I don't think I'll ever find anyone. Boys don't fancy me. Not the boys I'm interested in anyway. Maybe I should try to be more like the others? Be a bit normal. Get rid of these.' I tugged at the coloured streaks in my hair. 'Shop in New Look and Top Shop, listen to Justin Timberlake, be more girly.' I thought about doing those sorts of things a lot. Life would be so much easier. I could put a JT poster on my bedroom wall. That would be easy enough. Resisting the temptation to throw darts at it would be a little more difficult.

'What's wrong with being yourself?'

'That's pretty obvious isn't it? Nobody likes me. Not boys or my so-called friends. Why d'you think I'm sitting here on my own?'

'You're not on your own now.'

'You know what I mean,' I snapped at her.

She turned and looked at me.

'Never be afraid of being yourself, Nancy. But

don't hide behind it either. Speaking your mind is good, but only if you also know when to say you're sorry.'

'This time I haven't even done anything wrong. Why should I be the one to say sorry?'

'Because you can. And because, whatever your intentions, the outcome is something that needs an apology. It doesn't matter who's in the wrong. Friendships . . . relationships . . . are too important to waste time worrying about such petty things.'

She got up, smiled and started to walk away. She stopped for a moment.

'But if you say you're sorry you've got to mean it with all your heart. No half measures. Though I doubt you do anything by half.' She smiled once more and then headed back down the path.

It was then I realized who she had been reminding me of all this time. It made me giggle to think of it. It was Yoda, though taller and not as green, but equally full of wise advice and teachings and never losing her cool. Did that make me the female version of Luke Skywalker? Did she see in me the risk of going over to the dark side? I wasn't sure I could follow her path, though. Saying sorry when it was the other person's fault? Did that really work? What if the other person threw it back in your face? But if they did that it would make them feel pretty bad. Or maybe they'd just laugh at you instead and I was plenty fed up of being laughed at.

Sarah

The first sign that things were going wrong was when the train pulled into a tiny little station that looked like something off *Heartbeat* and after ten minutes still hadn't moved.

'Do you think there's a problem?' Hannah looked at me.

Before I could answer, the carriage door swung open and a guy in uniform strode into the carriage.

'*Quittez le train, s'il vous plaît. Le train se termine ici.*' He gave us an icy stare as he marched past and into the next carriage. With much muttering and sighing the other passengers started to gather their things and head for the exits.

'What's happening?' Hannah clasped her bag tightly.

'I think we're supposed to get off the train.' I shrugged.

'Get off? But we've got tickets. We're going to Paris.' Hannah glanced at the other passengers now disappearing on to the platform, then back at me. 'We can't get off here.'

The uniformed guy reappeared, still barking the same instructions. He stopped when he got to us, the only people still left on the train, and, hands on his hips again, growled, '*Quittez le train, le train se termine ici.*' He wasn't a man to argue with, like some scary sergeant-major type. I grabbed my bag.

'Come on.'

We jumped on to the platform and, within seconds, the train was moving again, but back in the direction it had come from. As it went past the sergeant-major stood staring out of one of the windows.

'What do we do now?' Hannah asked, sounding totally miserable.

'Wait for another train?'

'And when will that come? Everyone else has disappeared.'

She was right. All the other passengers had left the platform. It wasn't a great sign that another train was imminent.

'Maybe there's a bus instead. I went to a swim meet in Nottingham once and the train was cancelled so they put on a bus to take us the rest of the way.'

Hannah brightened again.

'That's probably it. Everyone will be waiting outside the station.'

How wrong could we be?

Outside the station was a completely empty road. Not one single other passenger. Not one single other person. Just the road and fields. As far as you could see, field after field. No village, no houses. Nothing.

We both just stood and stared for a while. It didn't seem possible.

'How could everyone have disappeared so quickly?' Hannah asked eventually. I'd been asking myself that question over and over.

'I don't know. Maybe the bus came and went.'

'But we were like a minute behind them. At the most. A bus would have waited. A British bus would have waited.'

'Maybe there's someone in the station?'

'There wasn't a second ago.'

'I'll check anyway.' I went back inside, but there was nobody. The horrible feeling in my stomach, like mice eating at my insides, got worse. I suddenly thought of Nancy. If she were here she'd know what to do. If she were here this would never have happened in the first place. She'd have made the guy on the train take us to Paris. Or at least explain himself. She'd have refused to get off until she knew what was happening. Or, if we had been all been made to get off, she'd already have come up with a plan.

I went back out to Hannah.

'Nothing,' I said.

'I wish Nancy were here.' She sounded just as scared as I felt.

I nodded.

'What are we going to do? We don't even know what direction to walk in to find help.' It all sounded hopeless. We were in big trouble. If only we'd stayed at the château.

'No one knows where we are. No one will even miss us until dinner. We might never be found. Everything that happened with Nancy, that was fate telling us not to go and we ignored it.'

Was it fate or bad karma? Hannah went on about karma all the time. Maybe this was payback for Rhys and me and the way things had ended up with Nancy. I'd felt like my heart had been wrenched from my chest when I'd seen her with Murphy. But, sitting on the train, watching the fields blur by, I'd started to think that the person I should have been mad at was him, not her. I kept replaying the scene. That look on her face when she saw me wasn't put on. Even Nancy isn't that great an actor. She really hadn't known. The mice in my stomach gnawed a bit harder. I'd overreacted. Rushed back, spilled everything to Hannah, angry at Nancy and Murphy, but most of all Rhys. Everything had snowballed and now we were lost in the middle of a country we didn't know. It was my bad karma, my fault and up to me to try and fix it. What would Nancy do?

'We should start walking, we're bound to come to a house or a village eventually.' I looked at Hannah.

'Which way, though?' Neither direction looked hopeful.

'This way,' I said, trying to be as decisive as Nancy would be. I started to walk in the direction we'd come from. Hannah hesitated then followed.

It felt good to have made a decision. For about fifteen minutes. The road, which had looked pretty straight from outside the station, curled back on itself again and again like a demented snake. I could feel blisters growing to the size of golf balls inside my boots. It was like all other human beings on the planet had disappeared.

'I can't walk any further,' Hannah said after another half hour.

She sat down on a tree stump. I stood in front of her.

'What then?'

'I don't know. We're never going to find anyone just walking,' Hannah said after we'd gone round yet another bend. 'France is huge and practically no one lives here. It's much worse than getting lost in Britain.'

Much worse. Back home I could just get on my mobile and call my Mum. However lost we were, she'd be able to find us. Who could we call out here? We didn't know anybody apart from . . .

'We could call Nancy,' I offered. Even as I said it out loud I knew that's what we had to do. It was obvious really.

'What? No way. We're not even speaking to her.'

'We have to. She's the only person who can help. She can tell Mr Lang and he can get someone to come and collect us.'

'From where?' Hannah looked at me as if I was being totally dense. She was right. We didn't even know where we were so how could we expect anyone else to find us? 'And, anyway, she's such a cow she'd love it if she knew we were lost and probably wouldn't help us even if we begged. Which we are so not doing.'

But Nancy wasn't a cow. That title was mine.

'I think I might have been wrong about her yesterday.'

'What?'

'I've been thinking about it and I don't think she knew Murphy had asked us both out.'

'But you said . . .'

'I know. I was upset. But I've had time to figure it out a bit more.'

'She still shouldn't have gone out with him. She knew he fancied you and we'd both said we should try to get you together. She should never have decided to take him for herself. You don't do that to your friends.'

Hannah wasn't going to forgive Nancy without a fight. She'd believed me straightaway last night. Why did people believe bad things so much more easily than good things?

'But she knew I wasn't interested.'

'You told her, did you?'

'Kind of . . . she knew anyway.' This was straying into dangerous ground.

'I don't get it.'

And I knew this was the moment I had to tell her. Tell her why Nancy and me had fallen out in the first place. Tell her why I hadn't been interested in Murphy, but had then changed my mind. Tell her why us being lost in the middle of the French countryside was my fault. Tell her I was in love with her brother, that we'd been seeing each other behind her back and that now, quite possibly, he'd broken my heart.

And then my mobile phone started to vibrate. I pulled it out of my pocket and looked at the screen. It was a text, from Nancy.

'Who's it from?' Hannah asked. I didn't answer. I opened the text and read it. It said,

I'm really sorry. About everything. I made a mistake. Forgive me? I really want us all to be friends again. Hope you're having a good time in Paris. Honestly. Luv you guys.

I really wasn't expecting that.

Hannah

I read Nancy's text. And then I read it again. And then I had to look at Sarah to double check she'd read the same thing I had.

'I don't believe it.' I couldn't think of anything else to say. Nancy never apologized, not unless it was dragged out of her kicking and screeching, like Josh when he's going to the dentist. Not like this, totally out of the blue. It wasn't like her at all. Maybe someone had stolen her phone. But why would they? It had to be Nancy. She might have fallen on her head or something, but it had to be her. Sarah looked as stunned as I felt. And then she started crying, the second surprising event in less than a minute. I got up and put my arm round Sarah.

'What's wrong?' But she was snuffling too much to answer.

I didn't understand what was going on. Both

Nancy and Sarah were acting really weird. I'd got the feeling that Sarah had been about to tell me something before Nancy's text had arrived. For a moment my mind flashed back to the truth or dare game. There was no time to worry about them. We needed saving. My feet were hurting and there was a huge cloud heading in our direction. I wanted to go home. Or back to the château. Anywhere that wasn't a crummy old road in the middle of some muddy fields.

'Text her back. Tell her yes we're friends again and can she please rescue us.'

'Where do I say we are?'

'Somewhere near the five or sixth station we passed after the village. It was five or six stations we passed, wasn't it?'

Sarah shrugged.

'I wasn't counting.'

'I'm sure it was. Nance will know what to do.'

Sarah looked at me, then started hitting buttons. I didn't know how Nancy would get to us. I just knew somehow she would. Fate had made Nancy text us just at the right moment, so fate would lead her right to us.

Two hours later, the rain cloud had peed its contents on us and disappeared over the hills, it was starting to get dark and we were still huddled together on that stupid tree stump. I was starting to think that maybe I'd been wrong. Fate had let us down. Or maybe there was no such thing as fate. Rhys says fate is a load of rubbish. You make your own destiny. Well we'd definitely done a great job of making ours.

Then I heard a noise. A sort of rumbling sound. And over the top of the hedge I could see the branches of the trees being swung about like something large had strolled past. It was just like in *Lost*. You don't see the monster; you just see the trees being pushed over. I stood up. What on earth was coming our way?

Sarah stood up next to me and we gripped each other's arms so hard not even the world's strongest man could have prised us apart. We stared at the road. Two great beams of light bore down on us and then we saw it, squeezing down the narrow road. The coach, the same coach that had pulled into the school car park four days ago. I had to be dreaming. There was a blast of the horn that nearly knocked us off our feet and a rush of the brakes as it stopped right next to us. The doors concertinaed open and, even before I looked up, I knew who would be standing on the steps, in her Kickers and red socks.

'Anybody need a lift?' she said grinning. We

grinned back, and she leapt down the steps two at a time. We all sort of collapsed into a group hug and everything, absolutely everything, was OK again.